Love Shines Through

Memories of a wartime childhood

as related by

Jackie Fulton

Jackie Fulton

Table of Contents 2

2

Acknowledgments

My thanks to my lovely family who have helped me in so many ways. To my sons, Steve and Dave, who are always there for me and my daughter-in-law, Charlotte, who is better than any daughter, could ever be.

Also thanks to all my grandchildren: Charlie, who keeps me company after school each day; Trinity and Honor who keep me up to date in fashion; Sam with her children Tommy, Molly and Davy; Rachel with her kids: Ruby and Olivia; John. Not forgetting my 'big' grandsons: James, William and John.

Thank you, all of you: I am so proud of you all.

And special thanks to Eve, for typing this up for me and making sense of my ramblings: you were there for me through my dark days and you understood what I wanted to say and how I wanted to say it!

Foreword

This book started one day when I was telling a friend some of the stories remembered from my childhood. She said 'You ought to write it down'. My grand-daughters, Rachel and Trinity, had always told me that as well.

At first, I thought it would be impossible for me to do that as I'm not educated. I only became a confident reader when my sons went to school when I had the motivation to read so I could help them. But other people encouraged me, so gradually I started jotting down the stories as I remembered them and making notes as I went along. I talked to my brother, John, and he remembered some of the things I hadn't: it was interesting how we had different memories of some of the same events but we were able to help each other with the details.

As I remembered and wrote more, I realised writing about it was providing me with an excellent way of overcoming some of the negative thoughts I had about my life. As I wrote it became clear to me that, although all my early childhood was spent in the most awful surroundings, in squalor and in grime, my Mum had been the most wonderful mother there ever could have been. She faced the most appalling circumstances with true grit and devoted her whole life to us kids. We owe her everything and I dedicate this book to her. I also realised that, despite the many hardships and cruelty we endured, throughout it all we always laughed. Mum had a tremendous sense of humour which Sadie and I, in particular, shared: she and I were always hiding under the table, trying to stifle our giggles. As I've got older and mixed with different people, I have discovered that some of my friends had childhoods with a lot more material possessions than we had; they had clean homes and families where violence was an alien idea. Yet their childhoods seem to lack something that mine didn't: at least life in our family was never boring!

I've changed some of the names in the stories: I have no idea whether any of the families are still alive but, in order to avoid upsetting anyone or take any risks, I've taken pains to hide their true identities. The exceptions to this are members of my family who have given me their permission to use their names. However, all the stories and events I've related are true: if there are any discrepancies it's because of my faulty memory not down to artistic licence. As I explain, Pat was my half sister but in our family she was equal: she was my sister as much as Sadie was and she was always my role model. I am thrilled to have an opportunity to tell everyone just what a wonderful sister she was to me; similarly her husband, Cyril who was our rock. Our so-called 'father' is always referred to as: 'him' or 'he'; he wasn't worth capitals. Occasionally I've referred to him as 'the old man' because sometimes we used that term for him. To all of us, he was beneath contempt.

My story is one of tears and laughter; of abject poverty; of love and of hatred. Despite the hardships we kids all came through in the end, so it's a story of resilience formed through the love of one amazing woman: my Mum.

I hope you enjoy reading my story

Jackie

Jackie Fulton

Home

My story begins in Woodfield Place, Paddington, where Mum and the old man lived before it was bombed in the early part of the War: I was taken here after being born in St Mary's hospital.

After the bombing we were re-housed 'temporarily' within the same area: that was a poor joke as we stayed there for the whole of my childhood. It was part of an old Victorian house, splendid in its day, but by the time we moved in it was a slum tenement.

It was very run down, and had no hot water or electricity so, until I was sixteen, all the rooms were lit by gas mantle.

Our part of the house was just three rooms: the kitchen, which we mainly lived in, known grandly as the 'parlour', plus a 'front room' and one bedroom.

Downstairs was the scullery which everyone in the building could use but it was so horrible, we never, ever used it, apart from the toilet there but only if we were caught short.

My sister, Sadie, used to say, 'It smells of dead people' and I'd say: 'How many dead people have you smelt then?'

My Mum worked constantly to try and keep us clean but there was always a dreadful smell of dirt, damp and decay that hovered underneath. Grime hung in the air with its pervasive taste of squalor and neglect. However much my Mum scrubbed that fucking lino the dirt stubbornly stayed there until eventually the pattern came off. It didn't matter how many times the walls were painted, that basic rotten smell never went away; a nauseating, overwhelming mixture of stale cooking, damp washing, abject poverty and need. It clung to the furniture, to the floors, to the walls; ingrained dirt that wouldn't leave.

The whole place was unheated apart from the kitchen fire and it was absolutely freezing cold during the winter: there was always frost on the inside of the draughty old sash windows.

Then, to cap it all, we discovered bed bugs so we had to get the 'fumigator' to clear them; this was so embarrassing for me as we had to leave the house whilst he did his job, so everyone knew what was happening and just how vile our home was.

There was no privacy of any kind so everyone knew everyone else's business. This was frequently excruciatingly embarrassing for everyone in the house but especially so for us girls as we grew up. There were only two lavatories for the whole building and of course no bathroom: we had to have a bath once a week in the big old tin bath that was kept hanging outside our kitchen door on a large hook. Girls went in first, the boys next, all using the same water of course. When I wanted to retaliate with my brothers over some wrong I thought they'd done me, I'd say defiantly, 'I've wee--ed in it!'

Lovely!

We had two wardrobes: one in his room for his suits, which we'd never go to, and one for everyone else to share. Our coats were hung in the passageway.

In the summer, after our hair had been washed, we used to sit on the steps outside the front door and be with the other kids to let our hair dry. We all used to have such a laugh together. But during the winter we sat shivering while our towel-rubbed locks slowly dried.

And Family

There were eight of us in the whole family: Mum (Ella) and the old man, (Jack), plus Pat from Mum's first marriage, who didn't live with us, and the five of us other kids.

Pat was the oldest being thirteen when I was born; Mum had just turned eighteen when she'd had her and after Pat she had twin boys a short time after. Sadly they died within a few days. Mum then found out her first husband was having an affair so eventually she left him and then she had to go work to support herself and Pat. No benefit system in those days so if you wanted to eat, you absolutely had to find a job. She couldn't look after Pat at the same time so Pat went to live with her Nan. But she pined for her Mum and desperately wanted to be with her. She and Mum used to meet up every week in a café. One day, when Pat went in, she couldn't see Mum, just a blonde woman sitting there so she asked the blonde, 'Have you seen my Mum?' The blonde lady turned to her and said 'I am your Mum'. Pat hadn't even recognised her!

I'm not sure where Mum herself lived, possibly with a friend. I know she worked as a theatre usherette which was quite a sought-after job then. I often think that must have been one of the happiest times of her life. I wish I'd asked her about that time but I never did.

I'm the eldest of the second family and Sadie came along two years later; John was born five years after me and then came Rob, the following year, six years younger than me. Jim was the baby of the family: I was nine when he was born. The old man used to call me The Little Bastard: it was only by chance that we found out later that was actually true. I'd already been born when he and Mum got married. It was Sadie who found out by looking in Mum's bag one day and finding the marriage certificate. Of course Sadie couldn't keep it to herself and asked Mum about it. Being still quite small I worried all the time that I was the cause of Mum's sad life as she must have got married just because of me. Of course she denied it.

My brother John was actually born in the awful slum we lived in, with bombs dropping all around and with the constant fear of doodlebugs. By then Mum had gone through six pregnancies : Pat, me and Sadie plus the twin boys. John was born at home because that was the custom; although hospital births were being encouraged at the time, most women preferred to stay at home with friends and family to help. Shortly after John was born the midwife came in to show the baby to me and Sadie. Looking back now I can recall he was a very handsome little boy, with lots of thick black hair and huge brown eyes that he'd inherited from Mum, but when the midwife told us he was a boy, I wasn't impressed.

I said, 'Take him back...we only want a girl; not a stinking boy!'

The kitchen was the room we all sat in for most of the time: it had an open coal fire, a table and chairs, a cooker and a sink. The kitchen was regularly emulsioned and repainted, mostly by the neighbours who felt so sorry for us all. They used to lay new lino, but very quickly the pattern on it would wash off as Mum scrubbed daily and struggled to keep the place clean. As we grew older we girls helped her more and more because we could see how she struggled against all the odds.

There was a large guard kept permanently around the fire, for safety, to prevent any of us kids falling onto it, and Mum would use this to dry the washing when she brought it back from the bag-wash so there was always a damp, musty smell to add to the other less-pleasant ones. The air was constantly steamy.

My over-riding memory, one which will never ever leave me, is the smell of decay, damp and dirt. I can't watch certain films or TV programmes because it just brings it all back and it is actually physically painful to me. Now I've reached the age I am, I find it amazing to think we were kept so clean: our clothes, our beds, ourselves. Because of this I feel an overwhelming sense of sadness for Mum but never for myself or my siblings as she did her utmost to make life bearable for us. I find it strange that, although I knew how sad some of the times were for us all, it's always just the thought of Mum which brings on the overpowering sadness and makes me weep for her.

And it's maybe because of my early life that I've always been very particular about keeping my own home clean and tidy. It's so easy nowadays with all the devices we have: washing machines, vacuum cleaners and all the rest...and of course, a decent, well-maintained home to start with. I remember when I was only about five or six, I used to black-lead the kitchen range until it gleaned and shone almost to silver: of course I always ended up even blacker than the range! Mum was so proud of me: she used to tell everyone how, despite being so young, I was such a help around the house. Yet she never, ever asked me to do jobs: I did them without being asked because I wanted to help Mum and make her life easier.

From eight years old I also did all the bagwash ironing which was a weekly task. It took me at least a couple of hours and left me with very swollen, hot hands. The system, if you can give it such a grand title, involved two irons: one which I would be ironing with and one which was heating up on the gas ring. As soon as one cooled down, I would swap them over and use the newly-heated iron, replacing the cooled one on the stove to reheat. The irons themselves really were made of iron, including the handles which therefore had to be held with a tea towel or your skin would be singed. (I once picked one up by mistake without the cloth and dropped it very quickly causing a singe on our lovely lino, which upset me more than the burnt hand; after all, skin generally healed; lino didn't!)

There were no ironing boards in those days so I had to use the kitchen table which was fine for bed linen but made shirts extremely difficult to do properly. When I ironed his shirts, of course, my main aim would naturally have been to singe them or burn them to bits but of course I couldn't because of Mum and knowing what he'd be likely to do to her. Although I was so young, I became really good at ironing, so much so that, when Pat got married to Cyril when I was seven, I used to iron some of Cyril's shirts to help Pat out and Cyril bought me a bike because I did it so well. I also helped him with his football team. Pat and Cyril were like surrogate parents to us all: they were amazing.

I wonder what youngsters would think of these jobs today?!

In The Family Way

Between John and Rob, Mum suffered a miscarriage as result of a kicking from him. I never forgave him for hurting my lovely Mum and that incident only added to my disgust and anger. On the day Mum had the miscarriage, I was at home and the first I knew that anything was wrong was when I went into the bedroom and saw blood everywhere. At the time I was only about eight and I didn't know anything about periods or babies or sex so I was terrified. But I did know my Mum used certain things monthly.

When the foetus came away, I put it in a pot and kept it for the doctor. Then I asked Mum, 'Shall I get one of those things you wear?'

My poor Mum had no time to stay in bed so shortly afterwards, she got up and just carried on as normal. I'm not sure she wanted another baby at the time but I'm just as sure she didn't try to do away with it because of the sad story of her sister, Elsie.

Elsie had been just thirty-two when she discovered she was pregnant. This was during the war and Elsie's husband was away, overseas, fighting for his country, but, as was so often the case, Elsie had started a brief affair with a young man at home. It would be easy for us all to condemn her for this but who could really blame people for trying to inject a little pleasure into lives blighted by air raids and food shortages? But then perhaps in the present era no one would think anything of an affair like they did then.

Elsie was terrified by the thought of the shame of her situation and her husband's hurt and anger, so she decided to have an abortion. Of course, in those days, there were no legal abortions and things had to be arranged with a back-street woman who 'took care of things'. So Elsie found out the name of someone who could help and off she went on her own; as so often, it all went horribly wrong. The first Mum knew about it was when a neighbour came round to her house and told her that Elsie had been found dead, sitting on a chair, with her life policies all around her so she must have had a premonition she was dying. The fire in the grate gone out but Elsie and Mum were so close, it was like the fire of Mum's life had gone out as well. When Mum heard the news she let out a strange animal, primeval scream: I've never ever heard a cry like that from anyone; it came from the depths of her whole being. The whole affair had such a terrible effect on her as, not only was she devastated by the loss of her dear, youngest sister, she also had to cope with the knowledge that Elsie hadn't felt able to confide in her.

So I knew without a shadow of a doubt, Mum would never have tried the same thing herself. Even though she was the youngest, Elsie would visit Mum despite everyone being so fearful of him.

When he heard about Elsie's death, the only words of sympathy were, 'Stop yer fucking grizzling and pull yerself togetha'.

Mum was so very sad after losing her sister that she lost a great deal of weight and seemed to us kids as though she never smiled for a long time. That made it a sad time for all of us kids as well and it stays in my mind even now, almost eighty years later.

Sent Away

Sadly Mum fell pregnant again shortly afterwards but, instead of putting on weight, she lost it because of the shock of losing her sister. She wasn't at all well carrying Rob and when he was born, she suffered a stroke and as a consequence, lost her memory. She was taken into hospital leaving us three children in the care of him. Of course it didn't fit his plans to look after three of us kids without help so he arranged for us to be taken into Children's Homes. At the time, such Homes weren't kindly places so all the neighbours rallied round and wanted to look after us instead. But he wouldn't hear of it.

The first inkling I had was when a strange woman came to the house and took John.

'Where are you taking my brother?'

'I'm taking him to look after him', she said.

The next day he called Sadie and me.

'Pack some bits; you're going on holiday'.

But I knew we weren't going on holiday and I told him we wouldn't go. For one thing we wanted to stay near the hospital where Mum was in case she came home. It didn't work as the next thing I knew, we were being piled into a car with our small bag of belongings. All the neighbours came out to see us go and wave us off and everyone was crying, including Sadie and all the neighbours. I didn't cry: I was determined not to let anyone know how scared and upset I was. There were no tears from him of course.

When we arrived at the Children's Home, Sadie burst into tears:

'I want my Mum', and she clung onto me.

She was the pretty one with the straight blonde hair: I had black, curly hair and I never smiled so no one seemed to take any notice of me except to criticise. Now I can see that's probably why I've always felt so angry against the world and I've never lost that anger. Even today I flare up quickly whenever I see someone being bullied. I may have been rough and gobby but I have never, ever bullied anyone.

They weren't kind to us in the Home. We were put into a dormitory with long rows of beds. Our beds were side by side which was the one redeeming feature but both Sadie and I had 'accidents' in the bed for which we were punished with slaps. Once I was sick and although I did manage to aim into a bowl, I got another resounding slap on the leg. Sadie sometimes messed the bed and was spitefully put under a shower to be hosed down without anyone testing the temperature. so it was generally either too hot too cold.

No one came to see us all the time were there and I felt forgotten and upset. I kept hoping one of the neighbours would come but no one did. I found out later that he'd refused to tell anyone where we were, even though they constantly asked him.

When at last we came out after six long months, I had lost so much weight that I was gaunt and pale. Sadie had developed mumps and had a swollen face and because of this she looked fat and well-fed next to me!

When we arrived back at our house Mum was waiting on the steps and she burst into tears when she saw us especially when she saw I was so weak I couldn't even walk up the stairs.

I've never really recovered from the trauma of being split up from Mum, from the lack of love at the Home, or from the feeling of complete abandonment by everyone and everything I held dear.

When we came back home to Mum, Sadie was such an easy girl to love, and I wasn't so I was pissed off with life even at such an early stage. After that the only people I showed any love to were Mum and Sadie.

Childhood and War

Much of my childhood was dominated in some way by the War. It's difficult to describe an environment where bombs are dropping all the time and everywhere you look, all round, there are bombed-out buildings with debris lying across the landscape. Raw spaces in terraced houses gaped like open wounds yet normal life carried on all around them. Life must have seemed very precarious I suppose to most of the adults but, as kids, we didn't really worry at all. We enjoyed playing on the bombsites, climbing the uncovered staircases and hiding in the rubble. We weren't at all scared of hurting ourselves of course.

Every time the air raid siren went off we all rushed to the shelter and that seemed quite a lot of fun until one night the shelter itself got hit. My Mum threw herself over us to protect us and we all managed to escape unhurt, but after that, whenever we heard the siren, to the huge disappointment of all us kids, we just stayed in the house.

One day, I decided I wanted chips so off I went to the chip shop but on the way the sirens started. I carried on. A warden saw me and yelled, 'Get into that shelter'.

I glanced at him then carried on towards the fish and chip shop. He yelled again and came rushing over to me.

20

'Get into that shelter – NOW! I said'.

'No, I want some chips'.

'You'll get more than fucking chips if you don't get in that shelter!' he retorted.

But one memory sticks in my mind about the shelter and that was the man who used to sing, always the same song, over and over:

Little man, you're cryin', I know why you're blue
Someone took your kiddy-car away
You better go to sleep now
Little man, you've had a busy day

Whenever something reminds me and that memory comes to the surface of my thoughts I'm taken straight back to that shelter and the sound of bombs dropping all around. And I always used to sing it to my grand-daughter, Trinity, when she was two or three years old.

During the war years, whenever you said goodbye to friends and family you could never be certain you'd see them again. One day, my Mum was sitting on the outside steps drying her hair when along came the rag and bone man calling, 'Any old iron? Any old iron?'

Mum was very surprised to see him as she hadn't seen him for a while so she laughingly said: 'Hello! I thought you were dead!'

'Me dead? No I ain't fucking dead', he replied crossly as he went off in disgust!

Evacuees

But after a while the bombing became more severe and deaths were getting to be commonplace so Mum was advised to send us kids off as evacuees. There was no way that she'd let us go on our own again after hearing about the Children's Home so she insisted on going too. Thinking about it now, I can see she was probably really pleased to have an excuse to leave the old man for a time.

We travelled down to a Somerset village on the train; on the way we shared a carriage with a lady and her little girl. The little girl was playing with two dolls, both with a porcelain face and both dressed in, to my eyes at least, the most beautiful dresses. Seeing me looking, eventually the lady said:

'Do you have a dolly?'

I said, 'No, I've never had one'.

She said to the little girl, 'Give her one of yours'.

To my amazement, the little girl did!

I was so thrilled with that doll and kept it with me all the time: that is until Sadie threw it out of the pram one day and broke it! I was heartbroken as I'd never ever had such a beautiful possession before (and not for a long time after).

We were housed us in a cottage attached to the school. This had an inside toilet, a treat unknown to us, and a separate bedroom for Sadie and me so it seemed like Paradise to us. That was the only time we had our own bedroom until we each got married. When we first arrived all the villagers laughed at us because we were so ignorant of rural life. I didn't even know what a cow was until a kindly farmer took me into the cowshed and showed me how to milk them. I thought it was amazing there: I even liked the smell of the cowpats! But we had no money when we arrived so, desperate to buy food, Mum eventually asked a local priest for help.

He refused saying, 'No, we're not a charity'.

I've never forgotten his lack of compassion and I've borne a grievance towards the Church from that day to this, even though one of my sons, and my nephew, both took holy orders and became priests.

Eventually we were given five shillings for food and after that we managed very well, until the old man demanded we return to London, presumably as he'd become tired of looking after himself; either that or he needed someone to beat up again. So back we went.

I really think the months we spent with Mum living in that Somerset village made up one of the happiest times of my whole life either before or after.

Him – the Man I Hated

The old man dominated the household with his violence. He had a nickname that all his mates called him – Mousie. This was a total misnomer as anyone less mousy than him would be hard to find. One of his partners in crime, (I use that term literally), was called Fairy: he was a big burly chap who terrified everyone he came into contact with. As in those days 'fairy' was considered quite an insult, no one could ever understand how or why he'd ever acquired the name or, even more, how anyone would dare use it. But to all and sundry that was the name he went by and I've no idea to this day what his real name was.

Although we lived in a tenement with just three rooms and a lavatory we shared with the tenants downstairs, the old man was never short of money. He only wore the finest clothes: a Cromby overcoat, the best leather shoes, lots of nice ties and always a hat. He drove a big, flashy car, one of the few in our street. But my Mum had very no nice things to wear and this used to incense me.

One day I was so cross about it.

'My Mum's only got two dresses and no nice warm clothes like you have', I told him.

24

To my huge surprise, he disappeared and returned a few hours later carrying a large parcel which he dumped at Mum's feet.

'There you are!' he snorted, staring at me.

Mum opened it and took out a grey mohair coat. Although it was beautiful, she never, ever liked it and I can never remember her wearing it. Consequently she used to lend it to me until in the end she gave it me. Obviously we had to keep that a secret from him.

I'm not sure why she didn't like it: perhaps because she didn't choose it, or perhaps she suspected it had been stolen. He associated with all sorts of dodgy people, mostly connected with the criminal fringes, and his income came from being a 'fence' for stolen goods. He also had connections working in a betting shop, and a stall outside a pub called The Green Man in the Edgeware Road. My brother John worked there on a Saturday from the age of twelve, even though he was supposed to be at school.

Even his own mother had no time for him.

'Your Dad's a bad seed', she constantly told us.

His sister Queenie wore a chain round her ankle which in those days was a sign of a prostitute, and he used to tell her: 'You've got too much make-up on; you'd better watch yourself.'

But he himself had friends who were 'on the game' as we used to call it. One day, he took me and Sadie round to a house which belonged to two of them. Business must have been thriving as they lived in a beautiful apartment which smelt really fragrant. I hated going there but Sadie was always keen.

'You never know, Jackie, they might have some nice clothes to give us', she suggested.

But we never got any! I've always wondered how he was involved with them: as a customer, a friend, or even as their pimp? Nothing would surprise me about him.

He was always extremely volatile and violent towards my Mum, so much so that I used to go to bed fully clothed in case I needed to run to the police station in the night. This was a fairly frequent occurrence so the local bobbies got to know me very well. The trip involved running across several main roads and was usually in the early hours of the morning: a horrifying scene by today's standards when kids are hardly allowed out during the day.

I remember one occasion vividly.

He came home, drunk as usual, and within a short time viciously set upon my poor Mum. I leapt out of bed, pulling on a jumper, and shot out the door, haring towards the police station as fast as I could go so he would have the least amount of time to wreak physical damage.

'He's hitting my Mummy again', I shouted as I burst through the station doorway trying desperately to see over the counter as I was much too short to reach up that high. One of the policemen had a young daughter about my age and he knew what had been going on, so he picked me up and put me in a Black Maria with another policeman, drove off to our house and burst in. The old man, of course, was still in a totally alcoholic state.

'What you gonna do abaht it then?' he mocked.

Whereupon they grabbed him and knocked the shit out of him. Then they arrested him and locked him in the cells for the night. It didn't have any lasting effect.

When he came back very early the next morning, Mum, Sadie and I were still in bed, with a sock keeping the door shut as it was broken. As soon as we heard the key in the lock, we all said 'Oh no, here it comes'

He put his bruised, punched, bloodied face round the door and snarled, 'You rats!'

He must have been a bit too tired to hit us all at that point and at least we all got the satisfaction of seeing him the target of the punches for once.

Boxing Day

I'm not sure how old I was but I do know I was very young and Sadie was even younger of course, when Mum was admitted to hospital with pneumonia.

My sister Pat was a young Mum by then and lived in Kilburn Lane, quite near us.

It was the day after Christmas. The old man wanted to go out so he put us to bed in the big bed which was his and Mum's and ordered us to stay in bed, not to go out of the room and to be quiet.

We had no food to eat and I don't remember having got any Christmas presents.

I can remember hearing people walking past the window, talking and laughing, but we couldn't look out because he'd said to stay put.

Sadie and I cuddled up to each other to try to keep warm. There was no fire in the room; we didn't have electricity, only gas mantles, which we couldn't light and it was beginning to get dark by then. We'd been left on our own since the morning.

As I'm writing this I realise how sad it was but then it was just the way we lived.

28

All of a sudden I heard my sister, Pat, calling, 'Jacqueline, open the door', which I did.

I burst into tears to see a kindly face, especially my lovely sister, Pat.

She lit a fire in the grate and made us a hot drink. Then she ran all the way back to her flat to get us some food. I remember turkey sandwiches, mince pies, a big chocolate cake and a flask of delicious sweet tea. Pat couldn't take us to hers as I remember I had an infected foot so it was too painful to step on. He of course had known that when he'd left us.

Pat was so angry though that she went round all the places where she thought he might be.

'That wife-beating shitbag has left his young daughters on their own in a dark, cold room with no food and he's ordered them not to move from the room', she shouted out everywhere.

Pat eventually managed to find a friend who could help her so she came back, wrapped Sadie and me up in blankets and then took us to her flat.

As we went out I said 'Don't forget the food Pat: we don't want him to have it!'

When we arrived there were presents for us to open: we hadn't seen Pat on Christmas Day as she's spent it with her Nan and had visited our Mum in hospital.

It was a dreadful Boxing Day and one which I'll never, ever, forget.

John and Rob

Despite the miscarriage which came between them, there is only one year and one day difference in the ages of John and Rob so everyone treated them like twins: one was born on December 1st and one on December 2nd.

It's hard to believe but Mum had two prams for them and she kept one at the bottom of the stairs and one across the road, just outside Doctor Dunlop's house. Mum always maintained they were such good babes; no trouble at all. But she also had Sadie and me to help with them which we loved to do. In those days, of course, there were no disposable nappies, just the terry towelling ones which all had to be boiled up daily. Given an average daily use was around five or six per baby, as we fed the baby then changed its nappy, and this four or five times a day at least, Mum must have had to wash around a dozen nappies every day but she never, ever complained.

By the time they were aged three and four, John and Rob had developed a real bond and were so close they were inseparable. Despite this, or maybe because of their closeness, like most children they had their fights and arguments. These could range from shouting matches to actual physical attacks in which Mum used to quickly intervene to resolve the peace. One day, however, things became more heated than usual and developed to such a degree that

30

Rob ended up hitting John on the head with a big train engine. He hurt him so badly that John had to be taken to hospital where they put in a couple of stitches. When they returned home, John suddenly decided to retaliate by doing exactly the same thing to Rob who then had to have a couple of stitches.....in exactly the same place as John! To this day both of them still bear the identical scars.

When they were about five or six, they played outside whenever possible but they were such sods they used to get up to all sorts of things and would travel on the buses or walk as far as Hyde Park. They weren't always missed straightaway but, as soon as one of us noticed they'd disappeared, I was dispatched to find them. However, the police almost always found them before me and they were taken to the local nick and given cocoa and sandwiches before being brought home in a police car. It would often be about 8 o'clock in the evening by that time and we were all worried sick.

I suppose the police must have felt sorry them both as they knew the situation at home and of course we didn't have a phone so they couldn't let us know they were safe; in those days though we just hoped and trusted that they'd turn up eventually....and they always did!

Holidays at the Seaside

My sister Pat was thirteen years older than me and, although she lived with her Nan, was very close to us all. Eventually she married Cyril and they lived in a flat in Kilburn Lane about ten minutes walk from our house which Sadie and I used to visit frequently. We loved Pat's flat almost as much as we loved her and Cyril as they were both really good to us. (In fact Cyril became like a father to my own sons later in life.)

I remember one day her dad came to the flat whilst Sadie and I were there and he handed Pat an envelope: to our astonishment, and hers, it contained £500. This was a lot of money in those days and he gave it to Pat and Cyril for a deposit on a house. They were so excited, as were we all, and they found and bought a small place in Neasden. Mum and all us kids considered this to be a little palace as it had a bathroom, a garden and four bedrooms; I remember at the time to all of us Neasden seemed like the country compared with our street and locality, and we used to go stay some weekends, whenever we could manage it.

Right Right from the beginning Pat and Cyril always took us all, every year, to Jaywick, near Clacton-on-Sea, for a holiday. We really loved it there and looked forward to it all year, counting the days as the time for our departure to the coast grew closer.

The trip there in itself was interesting and really good fun. Sometimes Pat and Mum would be in the car driven by one of Cyril's mates and all of us kids would be in Cyril's lorry: this was large with deep sides that dropped down. On the way we had what we considered to be wonderful refreshments: a flask of tea, thick bread and dripping sandwiches to eat. People on the buses, especially those on the top deck, could all see us and they used to wave to us as they drove past. They probably thought we were travellers or gypsies. Of course - we all needed no encouragement to wave back!

We loved the journey: it was SO exciting and we were safe: Cyril's friend was there to keep an eye on us.

Cyril always rented a big bungalow so we could all stay together. All of Pat's family, including her cousins and family on her Dad's side joined us on the beach so there were probably around forty of us altogether. I remember we all used to laugh so much as everyone shared the traditional cockney sense of humour. They were such fun times and I recall them with a great sense of nostalgia, not only for the wonderful sense of freedom and enjoyment, but also for the closeness of family in those days. It's so sad that nowadays families live separate lives and rarely have opportunities to share time together; life's improved so much in material ways but in other ways we've lost that sense of family ties, community and the feeling of belonging. No wonder so many people feel isolated from society, especially old people.

Throughout my life Cyril and Pat remained staunch supporters of me and my family: my sons loved them.

Looking back I realise that I was so fortunate to have such a lot of laughter in my life - as well as the tears - as I have many precious memories to think about now.

The only sad memory I have about those holidays is that, when he got old enough to work on the stall, John had to stay behind to help the old man and never got to come on holiday with us again.

I used to tell the old man it wasn't fair and he used to tell me to 'Shut up'. I always enjoyed telling him, 'I hate you so much'.

Good Game!

One day, when I was about eight and John was around three, we were left on to play on our own. We didn't have many toys so we were used to making our own games up. This particular day I said to John, 'I know, let's play hairdressers!'

''Or right', he said innocently.

John had always had the most beautiful, thick, straight hair and I decided it needed washing and drying. So I stood him up on a chair in front of the sink and washed his hair with the soap we used for washing up the dishes. I lathered it up and then scrubbed his head as hard as I could. John didn't complain but he wriggled around as it must have been really uncomfortable when the soap went his eyes and made them sting.

Eventually, when my arms were aching, I let John get down from the chair, his eyes streaming; then I moved the chair over so he could sit down near the cooker for the next stage of my plans. He had no idea what a treat lay in store for him.

I wanted it to be like a real hairdressers, (though I've no idea how I knew what they were like), so I needed a drier. I looked round the kitchen hopefully and then had a brainwave. I carefully selected one of Mum's saucepans for the correct size and placed it on the hob, then lit the gas under it. The saucepan heated up quickly and, when it had reached a temperature I considered correct, I went to take it off the cooker. I discovered it was much too hot, so I fetched a tea towel to hold it with. I then plonked it down on top of John's head and pressed it down like a 'real' dryer. John screamed blue murder and I saw the skin sizzle all the way round the rim of the saucepan. Mum came rushing in immediately, took one look at John's poor head, and instantly put cold water on the burns. She rushed us to the doctor who was aghast at the injuries my brother had sustained. Sadly, although she'd acted promptly, the burns took a long time to heal and left a terrible scar all round John's head, one which remains to this day, seventy years later.

A few months later, we were at a loose end again one day and were looking for something to play with.

'What shall we play?', I said.

And John replied: 'I don't know Lin, but I ain't playing no fuckin' 'airdressers'.

However, a few years later John got his revenge.

I'd thought of yet another 'good game' which involved John and Rob standing barefoot in front of me while I threw darts towards them, intending obviously to miss hitting them but to stick the lino around their toes instead.

They took their shoes and socks off reluctantly and then stood some distance away.

'Come nearer'', I demanded.

They edged forward.

'No nearer'.

Reluctantly they came towards me a bit more and I threw the darts.

Without warning, John picked one of them up and threw it directly into my right foot.

'Is that near enough now?', he asked as I yelled in pain and leapt around the floor in agony

John remembers that incident to this day as a source of great pride!!

Going to the Pub to be Paraded

Whmen Sadie and I were still quite little girls, the old man would take us to his pub just off the Edgeware Road, the White Horse, I believe it was called. We had no choice, we had to go and we grew to resent it as we were made to wear our prettiest dresses and our watches and our rings. This was, of course, for the sole purpose of making him look good in front of his cronies.

We would sit, sulky and bored for a couple of hours or so and all his mates would give us money: half crowns, (which at the time could buy a gallon of petrol), even fivers, all trying to look the most generous and well-off.

We'd always end up with so much money! Eventually, when either he'd tired of us or he wanted to do some 'business', we would be put in a taxi-cab and sent home.

Every time, when he came home late in the afternoon, he would demand all the money we'd been given. He didn't need it: he always had plenty, all earned from his criminal activities, but he knew we'd pass it on to Mum and he was determined she wouldn't have a penny of it. We were just as determined she would have it!

By this time in our lives, as young as we were, we'd got the measure of him so we'd give him half the money and put the rest in a small handbag. Then, when the coast was clear, we handed it over to Mum and we'd all enjoy a pie and mash tea.

He never, ever knew and that made it even better.

Scandal in the Street

Mum had a best friend called Glad and she and Mum spent a great deal of time together. Glad had one brother who was married with two children; he'd been in the army and been sent to fight overseas so Glad had supported her sister-in-law as people did during those dark days.

Just before the end of the War everyone in the whole street started gossiping: Glad's brother's wife had committed adultery with an American soldier. The strange thing was, it wasn't the adultery that people found unacceptable but the fact that the soldier was black. When I was a child I don't remember seeing anyone who was black and in those days it wasn't the done thing to have a black boyfriend. I didn't understand at the time why this was the case, and obviously now everyone is horrified by such prejudice but back then, because there were no black people around: that was just the way it was. No harm was meant by it; it was just the unknown.

Glad's sister-in-law left: I'm not sure even now whether she couldn't bear the shame of being an outcast in her own neighbourhood or because actually she went off with the American. Glad's brother brought up his children on his own: with everyone helping out of course.

I did see Glad's sister-in-law one evening: she was dancing in the street with the American soldier. I didn't say anything, though, because, whether you were adult or child, no one ever told tales on anyone else.

Attempted Patricide

My Mum was the most amazing, patient, forbearing, patient, long-suffering, stoic, tolerant, uncomplaining woman you could ever hope to meet. She loved all of us kids dearly and would have done anything to make our lives more bearable. This frequently meant she took punishments that would otherwise have fallen to us.

One day, when I was about seven years old and Sadie five, he lay into Mum, hitting her for well over half an hour and ranting at her all that time and more. We could hear the shouting and the thumps falling but, as children, we were powerless to intervene and try to bring an end to it. So instead we decided to plot his demise.

We thought of all the various methods we could use but it had to be practically possible so that meant using something we could get our hands on easily. That ruled out guns or knives, although I'm certain any number of his cronies could have facilitated the provision of either of those. We thought for some time and then eventually we settled on a method.

We found a piece of broken glass and a newspaper, which we folded and then we placed the glass between the papers. Sadie fetched an empty milk bottle to use as a rolling pin. We rolled this enthusiastically across the paper, over and over again, until the glass was ground down into a white powder, which I poured into a small envelope, waiting for the most appropriate time to use it.

The following day, he arrived home at his normal time and ordered his tea. I saw a golden opportunity to carry out my lethal plans.

'You sit down; I'll do it!' I shouted to Mum.

I then leaped up with alacrity before my plans could be foiled.

I retrieved the envelope containing the powdered glass, made his tea, and then poured the entire contents of the envelope into the cup. Then we sat there, my lovely little sister and me, watching him slurp the tea down in the disgusting manner he always used, loudly belching when he'd finished. He must have suspected something was afoot.

'What you two fucking lookin' at?', he snarled.

'A dead man, hopefully!' I was tempted to say.

We sat there, two little girls, expectantly waiting for him to fall forwards and die in front of us; instead he drank the tea then went downstairs to use the toilet. Sadie and I looked at each other, so disappointed. Looking back, I suppose the only explanation is that I'd lost most of the powdered glass out of the envelope as surely he couldn't have survived otherwise? Unfortunately we were daft enough to tell Mum who made us promise we'd never try anything again. I'm certain to this day she was only concerned for our future well-being, not for any wish to prolong his mortal life.

It does at least prove the saying 'Only the good die young' as certainly the bad didn't!!

Sunday Roast

From the age of seven I had to take a bus from the bottom of Sherland Road to the Edgeware Road to go to a particular butchers. This was one that he knew, and I always had to collect a large leg of lamb which Mum would then roast for our Sunday lunch. We would all look forward to this weekly treat but though we were all ready to sit down and eat at lunchtime, we would have to wait around, hungry, until he came turned up around 4 o'clock, before we could tuck in. However, although we grumbled amongst ourselves, it was worth waiting for as we always enjoyed roast potatoes, Yorkshire pudding with lots of vegetables and the most fabulous gravy imaginable. He allocated himself the task of carving it and, as he was always worse the wear for drink, we all prayed the knife would slip and he'd cut himself; sadly he never ever did.

Despite the size of the joint being substantial, he would invariably carve massive slices for himself then tiny cubes for each of us, including Mum. It was such an ordeal having to sit at the table with him as there was always a very tense atmosphere and he chomped and slurped his way through the entire meal.

44

As we got older things improved dramatically as we were eventually allowed to eat at 2 o'clock and his was put in the oven to keep warm.

One Sunday he was sitting at the table under the gaslight which was always on as the kitchen was permanently gloomy. Suddenly he yelled at Mum

'Put something on this bloody arm'. He'd had an abrasion which he'd neglected to the extent that it had become infected. Mum found the tin of poultice and put it into a saucepan of boiling water to heat up, and she also found some bandages. I offered to do the dressing as Mum wanted to get on with the washing up. I carefully placed some poultice on the bandage, the care being to prevent myself from getting burnt not on any account of his welfare. I knew the way to put a poultice on was to ensure the actual paste stayed on the top of the dressing so it didn't come into contact with the skin. It was a pure accident (though if I'd thought about it beforehand I would definitely have done it on purpose), but I put it on the wrong way round and the poultice went straight on the skin. He screamed out with the pain.

'What the fuck you doing?!' he yelled and his screaming blew the gaslight out! It was instantly pitch black in the kitchen but he still went for me, even though he was yelling out with the intense pain he was in. Mum stood in front, protecting me but in any case, he was unable to lash out physically so he mouthed the foulest expletives you can imagine at me.

But I did get the better of him, even unintentionally....which made me smile for the rest of the day!! Just another happy family Sunday lunch!

One day aged about nine, I had orders to go to get the usual leg of lamb from the butchers but I was always sick of having to look my best for him to show off. Mum saved every penny to make us look pretty.

So I put on a dress that was much too small, probably one of Sadie's, and which had some of the seams stretched and the hem hanging down. To finish it off I wore a pair of old plimsolls and scraped my hair back. When I got the butchers he was waiting for me to take me to the pub to show me off. He took one look at me.

'Why you fucking dressed like that?'

'All my other clothes are in the wash'.

'I ain't taking you like that'.

So I went straight home, delighted to have messed up his day.

Mum said, 'Oh Lyn, what are you like?' because she was so scared that one day, he would hurt me.

Funnily enough, he never did.

Ballet

When I was around seven years old I used to go to ballet classes with a friend of Mum's and her little daughter who was the same age as me.

I loved my ballet classes and I knew I was good: I was never a show-off but I knew I could dance - and so did everyone else.

I had a pair of soft ballet shoes first then, after a while, Mum saved up to buy me a pair of block toe pink satin ones. How I loved those shoes!

I'd dance around the kitchen for Mum, pirouetting and losing myself in my own world of dreams, miles away from the sad, sordid world I actually lived in.

Mum couldn't go with us every week so I used to go with Mrs Bale, as Mum's friend was called, plus her daughter.

Mrs Bale did a lot of dressmaking and was very clever with a needle so when the ballet school put on shows which it did from time to time, Mrs Bale was able to make all the costumes and was consequently a valuable asset to the school.

I was never, ever picked to dance on stage which upset me because Mrs Bale's daughter was always picked and I knew she couldn't dance as well as I could. In fact she didn't dance well at all. I knew it was all down to the fact that her Mum could make the dresses for nothing and she also had a very nice husband who would transport her around. Plus she had a nice home for the dance teachers to visit.

I still carried on dancing though.

The school wasn't an academy, just a hall used for all different types of functions. I realised that, because of my background and especially because of the old man's terrible name and reputation, I didn't stand a chance of being chosen for any special part.

I'm not one to feel sorry for myself or wallow in self-pity but, even though I was so young, I was aware of the 'haves' and the 'have-nots': that some people find it easy and others have to struggle through.

I still love watching ballet, especially Swan Lake, and many years later, I once went to see it at the Royal Albert Hall. I clubbed together with my friends so we could pay for a limo and a box in the Circle with an amazing view. I enjoyed that evening so much but, even so, I was so tearful that night after watching the ballet: I went right back to being that little girl in her pink satin ballet shoes, pirouetting on her toes in the kitchen, in front of my proud Mum.

My Friends

We children were all friends in our road and we used to play in the street. One of our favourite games was rounders and we used the whole street for this as there were few cars. The only car I can actually remember at all was his flashy car: although he kept us all poor and gave my Mum very little for housekeeping, he himself used to dress up in the finest clothes and drove this car.

We marked large hopscotch patterns on the pavement and spent hours hopping up and down throwing our stones in hopscotch games we invented with quite complicated rules.

Lots of the boys played marbles but they bored me so I never joined in but I did join them when they tied a rope round the lamppost and took turns hanging on it and swinging round and round until we became dizzy and had to stop.

Another favourite pastime was skipping and we were experts at this. We could not only skip forwards and backwards with great ease, we could also skip sideways and bounce the rope between skips. Very often the neighbours would come out into the street and join us: they'd bring a long rope and swing it so that all of us kids could run in and skip then run out again. We had many hours of fun doing this.

We also spent a lot of time doing gymnastics: we could all do a handstand and flip right over so we ended up in a 'crab' position from which we could scuttle around with our backs to the floor, tummies in the air, and heads bent back. One day I was doing handstands up against a wall when a man came over.

'How old are you little girl?', he asked me.

I didn't answer but just then Eric, the husband of one of my Mum's friends, came over.

'Clear off!', he said to the man; then to me:

'You mustn't tell him how old you are: you mustn't even talk to him'.

Although I didn't understand the implications of all this and certainly we didn't give any thought to paedophiles, I had a terrific sense of self-preservation so would sooner have hit a stranger than communicate with them. My standoffishness and his reputation kept us all safe!

His reputation helped us on other occasions too. Once when we were playing out, the notorious Notting Hill Gang arrived. They grabbed one poor boy and tarred and feathered him: this meant covering him with tar then sticking feathers all over it. It was the most unpleasant experience as it involved hard scrubbing by the neighbours to extract the poor victim. But we were never touched – his reputation was that we remained untouchable!

Family Friends

We had lots of friends from all social classes because, although our house was a tenement slum, others in the road were genteel and kept very nicely. There was just one woman who worked in politics, who banned her children from playing with us, claiming we were 'too rough'.

In the summer we all used to spend most of our time outside with the other kids. We would always be laughing although we were such a mixed crew. The boy I was most fond of was a boy who lived next door called Roy Everard. He went to boarding school and, when he came home in the holidays, he was such good fun, a bit like Peter Cook, with his posh accent, taking the piss out of some of the so-called 'hard-boys'. I used to cry with laughing at him as did the rest of the kids sitting on the steps.

Although he only lived next door, his home was much nicer than ours: his Mum and auntie lived there, but also, in their basement was another nice couple. They were a really nice type of people. To us they had everything: electricity, carpet on the stairs and they all even had TVs!

Next door on the other side, there was Mrs Poole and she had mental problems. She had two children, Billy and Margaret and we often used to see Billy sitting in the kitchen with washing hanging on a line strung over his head and water dripping down on him. Margaret had been born with rickets, with a double set of teeth and with an extra toe and finger. It had been decided by the family that Mrs Poole would be unable to care for Margaret so she'd gone to live with her aunt. They also had a cat called Billy, who was wild and ginger and had a habit of doing a poo in an old pot.

One time Margaret came to visit us for a whole day and while Margaret was there Mum went down to the basement. Margaret was sitting at the top of the basement stairs so Mum touched her leg.

'Dat fuckin' tat got ma leg!', she screamed.

We all fell about laughing so much that we actually cried!

Despite this, all of us kids, without exception were kind to Margaret and never ever made fun of her.

It was very sad as Margaret died when she was about twenty-one and her aunt died soon after - it was almost like she lived long enough to look after little Margaret and once Margaret went, her job was done.

One time the cat had kittens in a shoe box so Mr Poole took them out and had them put down. I cried for ages and wouldn't be consoled as I hated anything being killed and I still do.

Disgusting habit

One of his more disgusting habits that we girls had to contend with, was that he always kept a po under his bed. This was also known as a 'gazunder' for obvious reasons and in our case, it was an aluminium container specifically designed for the purpose of peeing in if you were caught short in the middle of the night.

Because he drank so much, his wee always smelt disgusting and he peed such a large quantity it nearly filled the po. By the morning it was rank.

Even from an early age, Sadie and I had the daily job of emptying it and we absolutely loathed doing it. We took it in turns and, when it was my turn, I felt an overwhelming desire to throw the piss all over him and then finish off by hitting him round the head with the pot. As I did this loathsome task, I mentally rehearsed how I would carry out my plans. I was quite a strong girl and I know I could have done a lot of damage, but I also knew, if I did, Mum would be lined up for a terrible beating. So I took the pot out rather than taking him out!!

Also, even more disgustingly, he would do the same in the kitchen using the same pot which he kept under the sink. He'd turn his back towards the sink, no matter who was in the room, even any of my friends, or any neighbours, Then he'd pee into the pot loudly, put it back under the sink and command me 'Empty that in a minute'. If Mum ever reproached him, even mildly, he shouted:

'Shut the fuck up. It's my house; I do what I like'.

I think of myself of working class but what class would he come under: someone who showed no respect for Mum or his kids. He had many friends who were thugs and criminals but he was the most disgusting of them all as, at least they were nice to their wives and kids and treated them with respect. I was just a little kid but I liked a lot of his mates: although they were probably arch villains they were kind to me and respectful to Mum.

So he wasn't even of the criminal class as least they had some morals, even if dubious! He had none.

The War Heroes

After the War, there were many reminders: some of the streets where we played, a few roads away, were left in a dire state, no more than a bombsite. Lots of the houses were just skeletons with rickety, exposed, wooden stairs which we used to run up; some with big wooden banisters which we used to slide down. Rob used to jump off some buildings with an old broken umbrella as a parachute. Once he was unlucky and landed awkwardly breaking his ankle.

At the top of our road was a small parade of shops: newsagents, butchers, grocers, greengrocers, hardware store, off-licence, post office plus others long forgotten.

Even more poignant, were soldiers who had returned, shell-shocked and in a sorry state after all the things they'd lived through and seen.

There was one young man who would pass us and offer us a 'lift' to the shops. The problem was he drove a 'pretend' car. When we accepted a 'lift' we would make a line behind the driver, holding onto each other, sticking our arms out when we turned. We'd then all go into the newsagents on the corner for sweets.

We all knew and understood that the man was shell-shocked as he'd been a soldier during the war and had been mentally damaged....along with thousands of other men who'd returned. Of course, just as many young men or more never returned at all.

When we were given a lift in the imaginary car we were all laughing but we weren't laughing at the young man; we were laughing at ourselves for going along with it.

Apart from the car driving there was another man, also a War veteran, who walked along our street touching every single railing or wall and, if he left one out he would start all over again.

I think the reason I didn't laugh at them, even though I was just a child at the time, was because Mum told us why they were the way they were.

'Don't you laugh at that man; he's like he is because he went in the army to fight for his country and was willing to give up his life for you. When he was shell-shocked it left him like that'.

So to us they were heroes.

Whenever they appeared, Mum and all the neighbours would offer them a cup of tea, poor things.

Television and Hair Wash

As children we only had a gas supply in our flat: no electricity until I was in my teens. So, of course, when television came about we knew we couldn't have one even though he could easily have afforded to buy the telly and have it installed.

We were welcomed in to watch TV at any of the neighbours who owned one as , most people, were really fond of Mum (not him of course).

When Pat got married day her Dad gave her a telly: this was in a massive cabinet which had a really tiny TV in. We kids though it was great so we used to go to Pat's and watch hers whenever we could, including Mum of course.

At the time however, we seemed to prefer playing outside: skipping, hopscotch and rounders.

In the summer early every Friday evening, Mum would wash our hair and then we'd all sit on the steps outside so it could dry. This was common practice then: no hairdryers of course. (Except for the incident with John's hair and the saucepan!!)

All of our little gang got on really well.

Next door to us in the same tenement building as Mrs Poole, upstairs at the top of the house, lived a nice woman called Mrs Light and she had a son, David, aged about ten years old. He never came out to play with us because of his excitability: the only time he came out was when he was taken to school by his Mum.

One day he had to be taken to see Dr Dunlop across the road. We were all sitting on the steps outside as usual and when we saw him we all shouted 'Hello!' To our amazement and delight, the boy suddenly started rushing around and shouting, pulling us onto the ground. We were tough kids and we could see he meant no harm, just having fun and we weren't bothered by his antics, but it made us laugh hysterically and of course Roy started running around aping him. This even made David laugh. Then his Mum came out and when she was what was going on, she called him away.

It was such a shame that his Mum hid him away because of his excitability; I suppose he'd be labelled 'hyperactive' now.. He would have been fine with us as we would have included him in our gang and we wouldn't have dreamed of bullying or mocking him but Mrs Light was too concerned that we'd hurt him so he never got the chance to play again.

I've often wondered what happened to poor David.

Christmas Presents

By the time Sadie was around six years old, my sister had become very polished at practising a new skill, which was being honed to perfection: the art of swearing. I used to find it hilariously funny, although I myself never swore.

At Christmas we rarely received any presents at all and, if we did, they weren't ever nice as he would never give Mum any extra money to put towards them. Mum tried her best and did the laundry for Cyril's football club, washing and ironing the whole kit every week and putting the earnings by towards our Christmas.

Cyril gave us fruit and Christmas stockings so that Mum's extra cash could go on buying us new clothes. The only thing he ever contributed was a turkey.

However, one year we received two large parcels addressed to Sadie and me from a couple of elderly ladies who lived not far away. Like most people who knew the family, they must have felt very sorry for Mum and us kids.

Sadie opened hers first and said: 'Fucking 'ell; what the fuck's this?!'

'This' was a rag doll, taller than either of us, with long dangly legs, wool for hair, and with its eyes, nose and mouth embroidered on. Sadly these weren't done very well so the doll had the appearance of being cross-eyed and with lopsided lips resembling a permanent sneer. Mine was the same. Mum in her usual kind way told us it was an extremely thoughtful thing that the ladies had done for us and told us both off for complaining and Sadie for swearing.

The following Christmas didn't change - we had very few presents but we still enjoyed it because we had each other: so not many presents but lots of laughs. But again there were two large boxes with each of our names on; we were so excited that we opened them together. To our utter dismay and disappointment there were another two rag dolls!

'Fucking hell: not another fucking rag doll!' Sadie said and mum and I just couldn't stop giggling!

Episode on the Bus!

Just another little story which shows the kind of man he was and his outlook on life in general and on other people.

He would sometimes take the bus from Shirland Road to the Edgware Road and he always went upstairs so he could have a 'fag' as used to say. I suppose it seems outrageous today but in then everyone smoked and it was acceptable everywhere; in all the public places, including the doctor's surgery. In fact, it was not unheard-of for the doctor to offer a quick cigarette to his patients on occasion, especially if they were friends as they often were then. Smoking was accepted on public transport: seats on buses, subway cars, and commuter trains were all equipped with ashtrays for this very purpose.

On this particular day, however, his smoking wasn't quite as appreciated by one lady who was sitting innocently just in front of him with her very small dog on her lap.

As he lit up the woman turned round and said:

'Don't blow that smoke near my dog!'

He wasn't used to being spoken to in such a manner and was immediately riled.

'What d'yer say again?', he growled back.

'I said "Don't blow that smoke near my dog"', the lady said again, taking the cigarette from his mouth and throwing it out the window. He leapt up, grabbed the dog from the woman's lap and through that out the window after it.

The woman screamed and shouted at him, then looked out of the window to see what had happened to the dog.

Fortunately, by a stroke of good luck, the dog had landed on the shoulders of an innocent passer-by (who was probably as completely shocked as the owner), and had suffered no injury at all.

He was taken to court and fined £5, quite a lot of money in those days for most people, though sadly not for him.

The local press got wind of the story and had a piece in the paper, all printed copies then of course, with the headline:

"MOUSE VERSUS DOG: DOG ON THE MEND"

Mouse was of course his nickname and was infamous in the local community.

It took a long time before the locals forgot about it and stopped ragging him.

A Win on the Horses!

One night the old man came home really drunk but, for once, in a really good mood, well in comparison with his usual self anyway. He'd had a big win on the horses apparently: it must have been fairly substantial as he gave my brother Rob a five pound note, a lot of money in those days.

Despite that, as soon as the old man had gone to bed, Rob took the note and deliberately and slowly, he tore it up into tiny pieces. That's how much he hated and despised him.

Jim, my youngest brother, got off his chair and started to pick all the pieces up off the floor. It took him a long while and he was very careful to collect every last little bit. When he had them all, he went downstairs to the basement where an old man called Monty lived. We'd got to know Monty quite well as he was always pleased to have a chat so we kids used to visit him. James was gone for some time (about two hours). Then he returned proudly holding the five pound note intact, plastered with sellotape.

The next day he took it to the local bank and they assured him it was legal tender and therefore could be spent in a shop.

Jim spent it immediately - all on himself....naturally!!

The Old Man also came into a lot of money, not that I know the source of it, but it was THOUSANDS of pounds, enough at least to buy us a small house.

But he went through the lot.

He was in a pub one day would you believe, and one of the punters asked him for more money as he'd given lots away, including to the man who was asking for more.

'Fuck off; you've already 'ad some, yer ponce'.

The man jumped up, whipped out a cut-throat razor and 'chivved' the old man, meaning he slashed his face twice on one side of his face, leaving two long open slashes before scarpering.

His mates took him to hospital where he had all his face stitched up without anaesthetic, because he was so drunk, and they bound him up so he looked like the Invisible Man; then he came home.

When we saw him in the morning, we were intrigued.

'Pity he missed his throat', I said to Sadie.

Now that I'm old I look at my grandchildren and know they would never, ever think that of their father, so I'm bemused to think back how I was towards him and how much I hoped he'd come to grief. Nothing would have been too bad for him in my opinion, and I've never changed my mind about this, in fact, looking back, I wish him even worse.

On one occasion John, who was fully mature at the age of thirteen, 'chinned' him, got him out the kitchen door, and then chinned him again. He fell down the stairs and as I saw him there, I felt a little sympathy and tearful. That was the one occasion I ever felt the slightest shred of sympathy for him and the utter sense of shame I immediately felt for being even a little bit sorry for him is something that will never leave me.

'I'm so ashamed that 'm crying because he's hurt '.

'You're crying because you're human', Rob comforted me.

It's strange that we are so programmed to feel common empathy and sympathy for other human beings that we can have these feelings even for the most despicable of them.

A Special Teacher

I remember I couldn't read at school. When I was about nine or ten, the teacher asked 'You're a bright little girl, why can't you read?'

'He hits my Mummy every day and every night', I said, 'and I can't stop thinking about it and worrying about her. I can't think of anything else'.

'Well, if you'd like to learn I would love to teach you. If you stay behind every night after school, when the other children leave we'll see what we can do. I'm sure you'll soon be able to read with a little help', that lovely lady said.

So I told Mum and she agreed I could stay on at school; every day my teacher helped me to learn to read. I loved it, not only the special time I shared with the teacher but because she was so kind to me. We broke the words down and I soon got the hang of reading and was enjoying this new world of words which was a total revelation to me. But after about four months, just as I was getting along fine with it and starting to love it, my special teacher surprised the whole class with an announcement.

'I have some wonderful news: I'm going to get married', she said. 'Isn't that exciting? And what's even more exciting is that I shall be moving to Malaya to live there'.

All the children were surprised as no one had had any idea we were about to lose our teacher and she was popular with everyone. But I was absolutely gutted as she was my lifeline in so many ways.

As the time neared for her departure, it was all we children talked about and over the last few days all the children took presents in for her. I really wanted to take something as well but I didn't want it to be an ordinary present like chocolates or flowers: it had to be something really special. The problem was: I had no money. Then I had a brainwave of an idea. I remembered there was a broken gramophone at home in which he kept a stash of stuff – glittery stuff that I knew he'd got from burglary and from other thieves as he acted as a fence.

When I got home I waited till the coast was clear then I went to the stash and picked out the biggest, most glittery item I could find. It was a brooch in the shape of a tiger's head. I can see it now, vividly, in my mind's eye. It was sparkly all over and had green eyes and a red tongue. I didn't realise at the time, of course, but it obviously was encrusted with diamonds, and the eyes were emeralds, the tongue a ruby. It must have been worth a small fortune! To my child's eyes though it was just a very special, pretty, sparkly gift for the teacher I adored.

I sneaked it into my bed and kept it under my pillow all night, and then in the morning, I took it to school, holding it firmly in my hand to keep it safe. As soon as the teacher came into the classroom I gave her the brooch. She thanked me profusely and remarked that it had a safety catch, something I remember quite clearly. It was such a very ornate object, I expect she thought I'd bought it in a cheap shop, though where she thought I'd got the money from even for that would have been a mystery. I was just so thrilled to know I'd given my special teacher a special gift.

When I went home that night after school, He whisked all us kids into the room where he was sitting with various cronies. One of these, I remember, had a scarred face but they were ALL intimidating. He then marched us over to the gramophone.

'You come 'ere, you lot. You bin in there?', he demanded, pointing at it. His mates were watching us closely.

'Which one of you lot's nicked something? What d'yer take?'

No one said a word.

'I said, what did yer take?', he repeated.

Still no one said anything so then he started hitting us. Still no one spoke: we never, ever snitched on each other. Eventually he rounded on me; I'm not sure why: maybe it was because I was the eldest, or maybe because I looked guilty and hated him which must have showed.

Whatever the reason he seemed to know it was me. He put his face right up against mine.

'I'll ask yer fer the last time: what did yer take?', he asked again.

'A brooch for my teacher', I said.

'F..ing hell! Well you betta go round there and get it back then hadn't yer'. He growled.

'I can't', I said.

'Why can't yer?'

'She's gone to Malaya'.

He went to lay into me but just then Mum came into the room.

'Don't you dare touch her', she shouted. And to my amazement at the time, he didn't, but looking back I realise it was because his mates were there and they wouldn't have put with him hitting his kids. But I expect Mum got the beating herself later on, instead.

So my teacher went off to Malaya, innocently wearing a brooch that was probably worth thousands! I still wonder whether she wore it and, if she did, whether anyone remarked upon it, though but I'm fairly certain she wouldn't have socialised in circles where there was any chance of it being recognised. Maybe at some point someone might have looked a little more closely and realised it was of significant value.

Exams

When I was eleven, the whole class had to go to the main hall to sit for our scholarship or 'The 11+' as we called it.

We all trooped along nervously but when we got there I was called to one side.

'Jacqueline, come here; you're not sitting the exam'.

"Why can't I do it?' I asked.

'No way are you bright enough'.

I begged them, 'PLEASE can I still be with all the other kids and make out I'm doing the exams?'

'No, you're going with Miss Marshall'.

So I was taken into a classroom with Miss Marshall who happened to be the most feared teacher in the school, amongst the girls that is. Even she seemed to look at me in a sympathetic, sad way and spoke to me quietly,

'You'll still get by in life. You don't always need to be clever to get on'.

But I knew that was bullshit: I had been rejected and, even at such a young age, although I wasn't clever, I wasn't a fool either.

And I've never forgotten the shame of that morning or the unthinking cruelty of the teachers who'd decided my fate and taken away my chances, even though they were so small as to be of no account.

When I had my sons, I made sure they both had a good education and each passed their 11+, getting scholarships.

School Life

I was happy at Wilberforce Street School: it was not a rough as the next school I went to which was Amberley Road, but, had I been able to read, life would have been easier for me.

In those days, teachers didn't seem to notice, or even care, if a child was sad or unhappy. I was always kept clean and wore decent clothes, all down to Mum of course, but, looking back, lots of kids were very grubby or scruffy and some were smelly. There was another girl who couldn't read but she was very aggressive and used to walk out of school frequently. We were drawn to each to her and I got to know her quite well; I really liked her as she was very funny and never aggressive to me and she also had a nice family. Her Dad was as nice as her Mum and her flat, which I used to visit, was always clean with lovely furniture and carpet; they also had electricity! She was a very pretty little girl, coming from a good-looking family, and her Dad was especially handsome (in fact an affair, which his wife never knew about. Sadly he was killed on the motorway whilst helping another motorist out).

Her name was Christine and she was an only child for about ten years, until her brother was born, after which she changed dramatically and became much better behaved.

She even began to read....well before me of course.

Before her brother was born, the man from 'The School Board', an attendance official, would look for Christine for days on end. With hindsight I think it is more than likely that Chris was hyperactive and needed treatment but she never received any extra help at all: that was just the way of it in those days. All the teachers knew of my own circumstances but no one ever approached Mum to see if she needed any help.

Christine's Nan, Mrs Robinson, was a young grandparent and very, very aggressive.

She was known all around the area for speaking her mind.

'I'm from a fighting family and I ain't scared of no fucker', she was frequently heard to claim but she was always pleasant to Mum, who, of course, was the complete opposite to Mrs Robinson in nature. Mum didn't go out drinking, didn't smoke, and didn't gossip as she had too much going on with her own life.

I used to think it was a real pity Mrs Robinson hadn't married the Old Man: I was quite certain she would soon have sorted him out....if she'd had the gross misfortune and stupidity to have married him, but then she probably would never have been that daft because she was too street-wise!

School Friends

One of my friends was Shirley. She used to have a lingering smell of cooking oil which followed her everywhere so consequently she wasn't popular at school. She always had to look after her brothers and was frequently sick. One day our teacher, Mr Green, announced to the whole class that he had two tickets for a West End show and would choose who to take. We all hoped he'd choose us as this was a rare treat. However, he picked Shirley who was ecstatic. She was then asked to choose a second person and she chose me! It was a really memorable night out and I've never forgotten the kindness of that teacher Mr Green.

The next school in Amberley Road was really rough. My Mum however, used to dress us up for school and I had a proper gymslip and bows in my hair. Although I was completely intimidated by the size of the school and the fact that I still found learning difficult, as usual my discomfort manifested as anger at the least provocation. One day an older girl accosted me in the cloakroom and asked:

'How many kids does your Mum have? Six? So she's been fucked six times!'

I pushed the girl back against the rows of pegs, pulled her hair and punched her in the face. She had to go to hospital and I was hauled before the Head and severely reprimanded but I was treated differently by all the other pupils after that!

One boy, Georgie Shayler, used to sit next to me. He had red hair and came from a very rough family but I liked him and we became good friends. He was called Rudolph on account of his bright red nose.

One day he came into school and pushed a roll of banknotes into my hand. There must have been a considerable amount there and it was obviously stolen, probably first by Georgie's dad and then by Georgie. As he gave it to me, Georgie leaned over and kissed me on the cheek. My friend screamed and the teacher said:

'It should have been Jackie screaming, not you!'

Georgie gave me a massive padded card every year on Valentine's Day and he always said: 'Come out with me Jackie' but, although he was a good friend, I never did. I liked his impudence, but he was unkempt and rough: I was always clean and nicely dressed and I never ever swore.

When I was a young Mum I heard George died quite young and I was very sad - Georgie was rough but he had a kind heart and he really liked me. When I felt school at fifteen, he said Goodbye to me and I thought 'Actually you're quite attractive' but because I'd been to school with him for so many years, even though he was attractive, I knew I wouldn't have him as a boyfriend.

Fright in the Night!

The sleeping arrangements in our house were: Mum, Sadie and I slept on a folding bed known as a 'put-u-up' in the sitting room; the old man and the boys slept in the bedroom with the boys sharing a double bed and him in a single one. By then Mum was completely worn out by all the pregnancies and she'd had also been diagnosed with a 'tired heart'. She was told she mustn't get pregnant again or she'd run the risk of dying but she was also worn down by years of what had been marital rape.

Following her stroke in her thirties she'd lost, not only most of the feeling in her hands, but also her short-term memory. Mum's physical state was very poor. I used to get impatient when she couldn't do my buttons up more quickly but now I feel so ashamed as I realise she hid the true extent of her state of health from us kids.

I remember one occasion when she was cooking chips: in those days every family had a 'chip-pan' which was just a large saucepan with a 'chip-basket' in it. Solidified lard was kept in the pan and heated up when needed. One day, Mum put her fingers in by mistake and, because she had no feeling in her hands, she didn't realise she was getting burnt. We all screamed with fear when we saw it.

Our bed had three parts to it so that we had to be extremely carefully when one of us got out of bed as otherwise the whole thing folded up with us inside.

I was around 13 and Sadie was 11, when one night there was an almighty crash which came from the bedroom and which woke us all up. It was a heart-stopping moment as the bang reverberated throughout the entire house. We three tried to leap out of bed at the same time whereupon the put-u-up folded up suddenly and we were all pinned in it, unable to move. Of course we all collapsed into giggles, even despite being frightened still not knowing what had caused the crash. Eventually we managed to free ourselves and then we catapulted into the bedroom. To our horror, we saw that the whole of the ceiling had crashed down on the bed! We ran in to find the boys and check to see if they'd been injured but to our intense relief they were both unharmed so we got them out from under the dust and bits of plaster. Then we all went into the parlour where Mum made us a cup of tea. I was sent round to the doctor's to ask him to come and take a look at the boys' cuts and bruises to make sure there were no serious injuries..

The doctor arrived and gave both boys a thorough examination. As he was leaving, he remarked cheerfully, 'Good job Mr H wasn't at home!'

We all looked at each other and then Mum said, 'He is!'

The doctor stared at us then rushed back into the bedroom: at the other end of the room was the old man, completely covered with debris so that he couldn't move because heavy pieces of plaster and concrete-like slabs pinned him down. It was instantly obvious that he was so drunk he'd slept through it. So we just left him and went back to bed.

The following morning, when he woke up and couldn't move, he yelled, 'Why the bloody hell didn't you lot come and get me out?'

'We tried to but you just told us to 'Fuck off!'', I said which, of course, was a complete lie.

We all thought it was hilarious and laughed about it for ages afterwards, not one of us giving a thought to the possible fatal injuries he might have incurred!

Shame he didn't.

Tonsils

As I'd always suffered with earache and sore throats right from when I was very young, the Doctor eventually decided I should have my tonsils removed. At that time this was a fairly common operation, routinely performed if a child had frequent colds or tonsillitis: nowadays, people know that tonsils are actually useful as they protect you but then it was considered better to remove them so 'having your tonsils and adenoids done' was commonplace.

Mum had my younger siblings to look after and would have found it difficult to take me to the hospital herself, so a neighbour, Mrs Dybell, offered to take me instead. On the day of the appointment we went along to the hospital, me carrying my night-things in a carrier bag and Mrs Dybell clutching a bunch of marigolds to put by my bed to cheer me up when I came round from the anaesthetic.

In those days, when anyone had an operation in hospital, they were admitted the day before: these days you're lucky to get a bed even on the day of the operation! The following day there were about ten of us kids sitting on a stretcher, all lined up, ready to 'go down' to the theatre, as we called it, then one by one off we went.

The next day, when I'd fully woken up following the operation my throat was so sore I was given ice cubes to suck, and after that, ice cream which was a massive treat in those days. I couldn't believe my luck!

When it was time for me to leave hospital and go home again, he decided to collect me in his flash car. However, when he came into the ward where I was waiting, I refused to speak to him and just turned my head away, looking in the opposite direction and muttering, 'I hate him'.

He turned to the astonished nurse: 'She's a little trouble-maker, she is', he told her.

'He only wants to show his car off', I said, but I also felt very sick so I clutched my mouth and ran off quickly towards the bathroom.

When I came back I found out he'd gone. Apparently she'd told him that I would probably be sick in his car and gave him a bowl to catch it.

'Well get someone else to take her home then; she's not going to be sick in my car!', he'd said.

As he left, the nurse winked at me.

'Thank you', I whispered.

I waited then a couple of hours later Mrs Dybell came to collect me, driven by her son in his van.

I wasn't sick of course….when I arrived home mum had made me my favourite lemon curd junket and I managed to eat it all, all signs of nausea having miraculously disappeared!!

Hair, Eyebrows and Fashion!

When I was around 12 years of age, my sister Pat had her hair cut in a new style: the bubble cut. It was very short and, of course, I wanted mine done the same. My hair was shoulder-length and dark brown, with large waves. Pat's was just a curly but hers was blonde and the bubble cut really suited her. She offered to pay for me to go to the hairdressers but I couldn't wait, I was impatient to look like Pat so I decided to cut it myself and recruited Sadie to help.

We waited until Mum went out to the shops then I fetched the scissors, which were fairly blunt, and a razor blade and we set up shop in the kitchen, unobserved by Mum who, of course, would have put a stop to our antics immediately.

I persuaded Sadie to chop the length off, a task which took ages. Then I set to with the razor blade. After quite a while, it was finished and I was really pleased with the result: my hair was extremely short, cut close to the head, exactly how I'd wanted it. Sadie agreed with me that it looked good and I felt on top of the world, like I could enter a beauty contest and win!

Thus fired up with our success, I decided to go that one step further and, to complete the new look, shave off my eyebrows and pencil them back in with brown eyeliner pencil which was the fashion at the time. Sadie was very worried about this shaving of the eyebrows, even more so when it was done as the hair looked great but the eyebrows not so wonderful! However, it was done and couldn't be undone.

When Mum came back and saw what I'd done she was devastated. She'd always loved my hair and used to spend a long time brushing it for me. But as for my eyebrows - she just couldn't believe that I'd actually shaved them off as well.

When the old man came home and saw me he said :

'You looked plain before you got your hair cut and your eyebrows shaved; now you look just plain ugly'.

When I went to school the following day all the girls crowded round to have a look : they were so impressed that I'd done it myself and they all thought it looked good. However, when the headmaster came into the classroom, he called me to the front of the class.

'You're a pretty girl; why on earth did you do that to yourself?'

I was so thrilled that he'd called me pretty that I couldn't say anything in reply. Then he said: 'Now go and wash that eyeliner off immediately'.

I said 'No; they're my eyebrows'.

He said 'Yes, but they're drawn on so wash them off! 'So I had no choice but to do it. Pat showed me how to draw them on to look more natural and they looked alright: they also grew back quite quickly.

I never shaved them again though!

Mr and Mrs E

Two houses to the left of us, in the basement, lived a lovely old couple called Mr and Mrs E. They also had four chickens and, on a Sunday, Mum used to give them some of our leftovers for the chickens. Looking back I realise they probably used to eat most of it themselves and perhaps Mum knew that they needed it and it was just her kind, tactful way of offering them some food without hurting their pride.

The E's home was very clean but old-fashioned, with lots of interesting ornaments and sepia photographs, and Sadie and I both loved going every Sunday to feed the chickens and enjoy some homemade lemonade.

Mr and Mrs E both knew the situation in our house with him: everyone did.

One Sunday, we were at their house, drinking our lemonade, when Mr E suddenly said:

'You're both a real credit to your Mum: when you're grown up you'll be decent grown-ups just like her'.

When Mr E said this, Mrs E's eyes filled with tears and she explained how she would so love to help us but they couldn't as they were both old and frail. We told them we were both alright.

Mr E had lots of medals from the Great War and also photos of him in uniform.

I said 'I wish I had a Granddad like you, Mr E', and as we left, Mrs E whispered, 'He's so proud of what you said to him!'

To this day seventy years later, I can still remember that conversation so clearly and I still think of that lovely old couple who live on in my heart. If only we realised how much effect we have on other people, we'd all be much more aware of how we act: and would no doubt be much more careful of the words we choose.

Mrs P and Her Hat

Mrs P was our next door neighbour: she was a simple soul, very childlike and when she came into our home, Mum would make Sadie and me sit under our very large table as we always used to giggle uncontrollably over the way Mrs P looked. She had very short hair that looked permanently dirty and greasy and despite being short, it was always adorned with a multitude of hairgrips and clips each side of her head.

Then there was the way she spoke: Mrs P would say things like: 'There was a big 'coo' at the shops' and 'I went up to Picalilly' instead of 'Piccadilly'. Or she'd call 'Hopscotch' 'hockstop'.

So we'd have to stuff our hand in our mouths in order to stop ourselves from laughing out loud. However, we did always manage to be polite to Mrs P's face because Mum told us she was 'simple', a term then used for anyone who would today be referred to as 'having special needs'.

Mum said Mrs P was very 'well-meaning' which was shorthand for 'Makes a mess of things but tries hard'!

One day Mrs P was in our home when the old man came in early which was a disaster waiting to happen as Mrs P was scared of him (along with most other people except us).

My brother, John, also happened to be on that particular day. When the old man came in and saw Mrs P he said:

'Fuck off you!'

John stood up and said 'Mrs P is a friend of Mum's' and told Mrs P she could stay. The old man jumped up and punched John on the jaw.

At this, Mrs P ran off screaming her head off.

John took hold of the old man's shirt and punched him all the way down the stairs. Naturally, the old man got up again, seemingly no harm done, except to one eye which was closing up and promised to turn black very quickly (in our view - hopefully).

Once upon a time John would never have had the courage to stand up to him like that but, ever since having to spend the night in the shop doorway, John had turned from being passive to aggressive towards him. I had always been the aggressor but now it was John and that was far more effective as, even at the age of twelve, John was 6' tall and very strong.

Despite this, the old man still attacked Mum verbally every day even though he didn't dare lay one finger on her after this so all the 'good hidings' stopped which was an amazing improvement for all of us.

Mrs P was not equipped in any way to be a mother, not because she was cruel, but because she was just not capable of managing motherhood as she was merely simple. Mr P was a lovely man who tried his best but he had a full-time job so wasn't always available to keep an eye on her.

As a consequence, Billy Poole the baby, was left in his old, none too clean, pram with water dripping on him from the washing line strung over his head: my Mum eventually had to tell Mrs P she could use Mum's wringer to stop the drips!

Mrs P also had two older daughters: Margaret and Maureen; Margaret was looked after by her aunt on account of her disabilities. Maureen lived just round the corner from us, also with relatives.

One day I called Mum over to Billy's pram: he had been given a bottle of milk but the bottle had contained disinfectant and Mrs P hadn't rinsed it out so Billy was drinking a rather strange concoction of milk flavoured strongly with Dettol! Sadly Billy died before he was even two years old: I've never known the cause of his death but I strongly suspect the poor little mite stood very little chance of survival in that household.

A short time after Billy's death the P's had an eviction order on account of the house being so dirty and smelly. The day of the court hearing the concerned neighbours rallied round and gave Mrs P a coat and hat to wear so she could at least look a little more presentable. The hat looked like a tricorn favoured by Admiral Nelson, but Mrs P had it on sideways: she looked so ridiculous that Sadie and I, along with all our friends, had to cover our mouths in order to stifle our laughter much to Mum's disapproval.

The court decided that the eviction would go ahead. I've no idea where Mr and Mrs P moved on to and I doubt very much whether the story had a happy ending. It was through this whole unhappy incident that I learned from an early age that poor, uneducated, simple people are treated disgracefully by society. All the people living around (apart from him), were decent working-class people, living in poor housing after the War and none of us, through no fault of our own, had much opportunity to escape to better conditions of housing, health or aspiration.

Religion and All That

As a child I never believed in God, you know, the man in the sky that people talk and pray to or go to Church to sing hymns.

I still don't believe but I did really love it when the Salvation Army used to come along our road with their band.

They did all help as much as they could for people like Mrs Pools and they were always very kind to Mum because of the situation she was in.

There was a boy in our street called Johnny who had lost his Mum to TB (tuberculosis, which was a killer in those days). Johnny was only six years old when she died and he used to say 'My Mum's in Heaven'. The Sally Army, as we called it, was very helpful to him because they believed that as well. None of us kids laughed at Johnny and his beliefs because we felt so sad for him.

I liked the Sally Army because they didn't try to convert us or talk to us about God. After all these years the Sally Army are top of my charity list as they do so much good to help the homeless and children in care etc.

91

They used to let us bang the drums and march with them as they left the street: all of us kids used to trail behind them!

Earache

I must have been about 13 when, I woke up in the middle of the night, with the most excruciating pain behind my left ear. It was so dreadful that I almost cried out in agony.

I'd always had problems with my ears and had suffered from regular, intermittent earache but this took the pain to a whole new level.

After some time of being in great distress I started to hallucinate with the agony and tapped Sadie on the side of the head:

'Why didn't you tell me there was a funeral?'

Sadie woke up and looked at me in amazement: not only was it the middle of the night, but she had no idea what I was talking about!!

Then she watched even more perplexed as I did the same thing to Mum: tapped her on the head and said:

Why didn't you invite me to the funeral?'

Poor Mum thought I was about to pop my clogs and hence the funeral talk.

They could both see I was in massive pain and had clearly lost the plot so they called the ambulance which came a short time later and rushed me off to hospital, bells ringing, as was the manner in those days.

I was placed in an adult ward and was diagnosed with a mastoid. The doctor told Mum that mastoid could lead to a very serious infection called 'meningitis' and this in turn could lead to brain damage.

My poor Mum was horror-struck at this and couldn't speak to the doctor, being lost for words. However, the doctor attempted to reassure her and hold out some hope as apparently 'Penicillin' was available which would offer some chance of my recovering.

He said he couldn't believe how well I was coping with the high level of pain and I would have laughed if I'd felt well enough: I coped with much higher levels of pain every single day of my life.

I begged the nurses not to let the old man visit me because of the hatred I felt for him for what he'd did to my Mum every day of her life, but they refused. I burst into tears; not with sadness of pain, but with fury!

A doctor came over and asked why I was so very upset. I explained the situation with as much detail as I could, given the level of physical pain I was in and he said:

'Don't worry little girl: you won't have any visitors you don't want to see'.

After that all the other patients made such a fuss of me, not just because of my story, but also because I was just a child amongst adult women, and all the neighbours visited me.

Despite all that attention, when I was eventually allowed to go home, I was so pleased to go back to Mum and Sadie.

When I got back, however, he burst in in a furious temper,

'Why the fucking hell didn't you let me in to see you?'

I just said 'Because I hate you of course'.

He was quiet after that, quiet for him, that is, because I was still very unwell.

I'd like to think he'd learned a lesson but that proved to be a vain hope as he continued as before.

The Birthday Card

His birthday and on the shelf over the fireplace, one card all on its own.

No date to celebrate as far as we kids were concerned: we all commiserated with each other that such a terrible, cruel, insensitive brute of a man had been born into the world. I used to ask myself why we were fated to share our lives in his shadow?

Every year it was the same old ritual: one fancy, very ornate card appeared, glittery picture on the front; treacly, overly-loving words inside. I couldn't imagine anyone buying such sickly muck like this for anyone at all, even for the love of their life: it was so gushing it was embarrassing to read.

And every single year as far back as I could remember, it was the same without fail. I didn't understand why Mum couldn't see through hi and why she carried on showing such adoring devotion.

And every year I watched him open it, grunt a begrudged, 'Thank You', then slope off.

Suddenly, one year I couldn't stand it any more and felt I just had to say something.

'Mum, I don't get it. Why do you give him a lovely birthday card like that, all those stupid, loving words?', I asked her . 'You do it every single year; he treats you so badly all the time and he's just a vicious, cruel, pig of a man. I just don't get it'.

'I have to otherwise he'll go bonkers', she said, by way of explanation.

'I know he will. But even so.....'.

'Well, when he goes bonkers you know what he's like. He turns nasty. I'm not worried for myself', Mum said, 'But for you lot. So……. I send him that card'.

Then she turned towards me grinning broadly.

'I know you've never noticed, but that's the same card. I send it every year; I've sent it for the last fourteen years! He's never noticed…… and nor have any of you lot!'

And that was the way of it: we kids and Mum forming a team against the pig of a man who'd fathered us but who I never, ever called Dad. The man who shaped my life and that of everyone in our home. The man I grew to hate with a passion.

He knew how much I loathed him and because of this, he wouldn't look into my eyes because he could see the hatred blazing there.

'Don't look at me like that', he used to say, so just staring at him gave me tremendous satisfaction.

To me he was, and would always be, 'him'. And when I write his name I don't give him a capital letter because he's just not worthy of one.

Guy Fawkes

Whenever November 5th came round each year, my brothers, Rob and John, used to dress Rob up as an old guy and sit him in a pushchair, then ask for 'A penny for the guy.'

I hated Bonfire night as, although I liked the pretty fireworks, I HATED the bangers because they brought back memories of the War and the sheer terror of bombs dropping all around.

One year, Rob and John were on their way to the firework party, when two well-known bullies from the area, came along and looked at the old 'guy' in the pram. Rob was sitting so still that they didn't realise he was a real person and one said to the other:

'Let's nick the guy; it looks great; best one I've ever seen.'

They approached the pram and looked inside: as they were leaning over, Rob jumped up suddenly and screamed loudly at them. They ran off at high speed or, as John put it: Shitting themselves.'

When the boys came home and told us al what had happened, how we laughed! But what a good lesson for those two bullies!

John always did like dressing up so when he was about fourteen the girl downstairs knocked on our kitchen door and said:

'There's a bloke outside wants to see you'.

I went outside and there was a guy with an old overcoat, a trilby hat, and a moustache.

'Is he there?' he asked.

'No, he's not'.

'Is he there?', the guy repeated.

'Who do you want?'

'I want ....youuuuuuuuu!'

I was terrified and went to kick him.

The bloke removed his hat and his moustache and it was John!!

Another time, the doorbell rang and there was a bloke standing there with a distorted face. He said nothing; just stared at me. Slowly inching towards me. I got so scared that he took the rubber mask off that he was wearing and just laughed. I was so angry at him for terrifying me that I flew down to the kitchen, picked up an empty coke bottle which was made of glass, and rushed back and hit him on the head. I had to stand on tiptoes as he was quite tall. As they say, he laughed on the other side of his face!!

John also had a funny habit that I've never forgotten (and nor has he as he reminded me of it): he used to pretend to sit down at a piano and play it like a famous and popular pianist at the time, Winifred Atwell. Sadie, Mum and I used to watch him through a crack in the door!

Tom

When I was thirteen Mum was diagnosed with dropsy. This is an old fashioned term which was commonly used at the time, when the whole body fills up with water and turns puffy. Today doctors realise this is generally due to congestive heart failure.

Oedema, as it's now called, affects the lower legs and feet and worsens when the sufferer stands on their feet all day. Of course, Mum, having four children at the time, had very little time to rest with her feet up, so her condition quickly deteriorated.

Mum gained an awful lot of weight over a year, bringing her to over 16 stones which, being only 5'2" tall was very noticeable.

One day the old man came in quite agitated to inform us that his friend, Tom, had been shot dead. This was a terrible shock for all of us and we were greatly distressed as we liked Tom an awful lot: he was such a lovely man I'd never understood how he could have associated with the likes of him, even though Tom must have been a criminal too.

'I've gotta go to bed; I'm so upset and shocked', he said. We could see they were crocodile tears and he was just acting the role.

Mum used to say he should been an actor the way he could fool other people (though he never fooled us).

We all went to bed early that night and it was really peaceful for a change as he was out the way.

Even though he was out and the coast was clear, we all spoke in hushed tones as usual: we were so scared of disturbing him and giving him what he would consider just cause to hit us. Sadie said how she'd love to shoot whoever had shot Tom, but Mum was never as aggressive as we were in our manner of speaking, so she kept quiet even though she was just as sad and upset as we girls were.

I said: 'I'd like to torture the killer: I'd have him tied to a chair, hum the stripper music, then let Mum sashay in stark staring naked!'

Being so large, the picture of Mum doing this was so funny as it would have terrified the killer and we all ended up in hysterics. We were still giggling when he came home so we had to stifle it in case he heard us.

We all adored Tom but we had such a dark sense of humour, developed over the years through living with him and probably in order to cope with his cruelty, and Mum knew us well enough to realise that we were not disrespecting either her or Tom by laughing so she joined in and laughed more than the rest of us at the vision of herself nude dancing to the stripper music.

It's such a great comfort to me in writing these stories to realise that Mum knew how much we loved her.

When Fish and Chips Were a Hit!

Despite all the hardship and sadness in our lives, we did have a lot of laughs, mainly because my lovely Mum would always try to see the good side of life. It must have been so hard for her, all the beatings she suffered and I know she often took some on our behalf too. But she was always cheerful and, difficult though it must often have been, she would always see the funny side of things.

One of the incidents I remember really well started off at home but happened in the chip shop of all places.

By the time I was a young teenager, the fear and anger towards him had grown and by then I really hated him. But by then I also realised, although he could hurt me physically, he would never again hurt me mentally because I didn't have any respect for him at all. I knew that, as soon as I was old enough I'd leave and I couldn't wait for that time, although I was worried about leaving my Mum.

This particular evening, my friend came round and asked if I wanted to go with her to the fish and chip shop. Off we went and we were standing chatting in the queue when he came in. I was really annoyed to see him standing there, dressed to the nines as usual in his expensive jacket and smart shoes, especially as I knew my poor Mum never had anything new to wear.

I knew I was risking a good hiding but I couldn't stop myself and said:

'You know I hate you, don't you?'

The whole chip shop turned silent. I didn't look around but could sense everyone watching to see what he would do next. He had such a reputation it was clear to everyone there that he wouldn't tolerate being shown up in public, especially not by a girl.

I knew I was for it this time so I shot out of the chip shop and dashed home as fast as I could run.

'Quick, we've got to leave!'

My Mum could see the state I was in.

'What's happened?' she asked.

'Please come quick: I yelled at him in the chip shop and he's after me'.

Mum turned pale and we all scampered down the stairs to get out the back of the house before he got home. As we reached the bottom of the stairs, the big tin bath which hung on the wall at the top, dropped off its hook and banged down the stairs after us.

Mum said: 'See - even the fucking bath's scared of him!'

I remember we didn't dare go home all night but left the boys with Mum's friend, Glad, and we three stayed in a neighbour's house until the old man had cooled off.

I still got a slap in the face the next day but it had been worth it!

Treatment for the Flu'

One day, when I was a young teenager, Sadie and I were both at home when the old man returned unexpectedly quite early in the day. He did actually look quite ill even to my ultra-critical eyes, though naturally I felt no sympathy for him. He seemed to be suffering from a severe bout of the 'flu and, realising he needed medical help, he ordered me to arrange a doctor's visit from the surgery just across the road from our house.

'Git yerself across to that doctor's and get me some'at fer this flu. Tell 'im I feel dreadful', he ordered me.

'You'll be lucky!' I thought to myself.

In our kitchen there was a large cupboard which was full of old bits and pieces, but which also served as a medicine cabinet. The medicines in there were all the remaining dregs from prescriptions, potions and pills prescribed and acquired over the years. These all must have been, of course, well over their use-by dates, although in those dates these were never printed on them anyway.

Sadie and I took one of the bottles, washed it and then concocted a cocktail of all the very oldest medicines we could find. I then found a small glass and a teaspoon and took them up to his room. The room itself smelt foul: his flatulence and boozy breath had mixed into a toxic air.

'Doctor Dunlop can't pay a visit to you today as there's a 'flu epidemic going round, so he's sent some medicine which he says will make you feel better', I announced and I poured a couple of teaspoons into the glass. He took it, and then he told me to leave it there, which I did.

Over the course of the next few days, he took the whole lot. We watched him keenly, waiting for a deterioration in his condition but...guess what? He got better, the old bastard.

We all had to laugh at the ridiculousness of it all!

The Crashed Van

One late afternoon my good friend Jean called round to ask me to go out with her for a few hours. We took the bus to a milk bar in the Edgeware Road. I loved it there as you could jive which I was good at doing. As we walked into the milk bar, Jean recognised a couple of boys she knew and they came over.

'Hi you two: fancy a knickerbocker glory?', one of them offered.

This was a large ice cream with fruit, popular at the time and a real treat for us.

'OK, Jean said, grinning slyly at me at the offer of a free treat.

They bought us a knickerbocker glory each, and we stayed for a while jiving and chatting, all of us generally relaxed and enjoying ourselves.

After about an hour or so one of the boys made a suggestion.

'How about you come with us for a ride around in my motor?'

Jena and I looked at each other.

'OK then', I said, 'But I'll get a good hiding if I'm not home by nine'.

So we piled into the car and motored round various parts of London. I was watching the time as I knew the nine o'clock curfew must be strictly observed or I'd be for it and by then it was about 8.30.

'Er...I need to get home soon. Can we head that way now?' I said.

So we start making our way towards home.

We arrived at Jean's road first and dropped her off then drove on to my road. Suddenly the car seemed to lose control and veered sideways, slewing wildly across the road, this way and that, until it finally careered into a van parked at the side of the road. We were all stunned but to my horror I suddenly recognised the van: it was his.

The two boys immediately jumped out of the crashed car and ran off out of sight and I realised that the car in which we had been driving all round London in full view, was actually nicked! It was just fortuitous that we three were unharmed as the van was totally smashed.

I crept into our house as and told Mum and Sadie what had happened. Mum's immediate reaction was to say:

'Thank Goodness you're not hurt!'

Sadie, much more practical said:

'She still could be when he finds out!'

When he arrived home that night around 10 o'clock, he was so smashed with alcohol that he didn't notice his van. It was a different matter in the morning! He want down to get into the van, then came storming back upstairs saying:

'Some fucker's crashed into my fucking van.'

We didn't say a word. Some of neighbours knew it was me in the car that did the damage but no one ever let on: the law in the slums was always 'No tales'....especially for the likes of him!!

My Sister's Wedding

I left school at fifteen and got a job in a factory. The first day I woke early as I was so excited to be going out to work at last. I wore my best dress together with shoes that had very high heels and an ankle strap; these were the latest fashion and I felt good in them. I knew I was attractive with my fashionable hair and slim figure, and I oozed confidence. Sadie came with me and on the way up the stairs to Reception; all the boys whistled at us, which confirmed that we looked good and made us feel great! It wasn't like things nowadays when whistling at girls is considered a form of sexual assault: if you got whistled at when I was young, it made your day; in fact, you felt quite offended if you weren't!

I loved working in that factory as I liked the camaraderie and we all looked out for each other. But after a year I became anaemic so I had to leave. Sadie had just left school so we decided to get a job together at the local halibut oil factory. At the time there was a picture of Audrey Hepburn, on posters all around that advertised the oil, so we thought it would be glamorous to work there. But, of course, life on the factory floor wasn't so very glamorous and, on the very first day, having worked from 8 o'clock to noon without a break, we were desperate to visit the loo. In those days, workers' rights were unheard of and there were no comfort breaks so we weren't allowed to go. By lunchtime we'd left!

Although there were few rights for workers, there were plenty of jobs around. Factory work was considered a good job as it paid well and you could usually have a chat to pass the time away. Although it was comparatively well, paid, men earned a great deal more than women of course, even for doing exactly the same job.

However, life was to change quickly.

Sadie became quite secretive and it seemed as if she was staying out of our way. She didn't say a word to any of us, but eventually Pat said to me:

'I'm sure Sadie's carrying' (Meaning she was pregnant as that's what we used to call it in those days).

So she asked her straight out, 'Are you in the family way? If you are, don't worry: we'll all help out'.

So I made an appointment and took her to the doctor's. The doctor sat in his chair, smelling of gin and smoking a cigarette as was quite usual. His hands always shook as if he could hardly wait for his next drink.

He agreed that he thought Sadie was 'expecting' but prescribed some pills which he said would bring on a period. Sadie took them for a few weeks but nothing happened and so eventually Sadie and Eddie knew they'd have to get married. In those days it was the only thing to do if you were 'courting', and generally expected even if you weren't going out! Many a young man found himself unexpectedly backed into marriage following a one-night fling. There were few unmarried mothers as there was no benefit system to rely on and being on your own with a child on the way showed you were 'no better than you ought to be', a disparaging term to show the world's disapproval. So most young men accepted it was a risk you took if you 'went the whole way' with your girlfriend, that is, ending up with a 'shotgun wedding' as it was called, the picture being of the girl's angry father chasing the chap down the road with a shotgun until he agrees to marry and 'make an honest woman' of her.

Once Sadie and Eddie had accepted the inevitable and decided to marry, we all got quite excited about the wedding, especially me, and I started planning the outfits, particularly Sadie's.

She was desperately keen to wear a duster-coat. This was a loose-fitting coat and the latest fashion but it wasn't what I had in mind for her at all and, as usual, I got my own way. I took her to a very upmarket shop which sold 'debs' dresses in white and cream and bought her the nicest one I could find, together with a cream beautiful hat to wear with it.

I bought myself a lovely navy dress and a navy and white hat. We both felt absolutely wonderful in these clothes. We also dressed our little niece, Sue, up in a lemon dress with little white shoes. She was about four years old at the time and she looked a picture as she was a very pretty little girl with blonde hair.

I gave Sadie away: she didn't look pregnant at the short ceremony, although, when we looked at the honeymoon photos, it was plain for all to see.

Sadie and Eddie, of course, had very little money and, in any case, being just after the war, there were few flats or houses to rent, so they went to live with Eddie's family, sharing Eddie's old bedroom, until they'd saved up enough money to buy a home of their own.

And my first nephew was born there: Robert.

Accident on the Loo!

He had one sister, our Aunt Lil, and she was also our Godmother. Aunt Lil was alright but we didn't see much of her as nobody in the family ever wanted to come and visit us because of him, including even his own Mum.

My Granddad, who I liked so much, had remained in the flat he'd shared with my Nan before she'd died; it was a nice flat and also had a decent garden. Aunt Lil had originally had a flat of her own but she and her husband, Charlie, had moved in with Granddad supposedly to look after him. They had a television which, of course we didn't have, so I used to go round there with Sadie and see if we could watch some telly; usually we weren't allowed to though as we were always told Granddad had to rest. We knew Granddad liked to see us although we got the impression Aunt Lil didn't want us there as she never made us feel welcome.

When Mum died, Aunt Lil started coming round to do some household jobs and helping to keep the home at least in some sort of order. She always made a fuss of the boys but didn't have contact with us girls as we were married by then. If our paths crossed I was always very short with her as I remembered how she'd always made it clear she hadn't welcomed our visits when we were younger, so I generally never even bothered to speak to her, thereby treating her exactly the same as she'd treated us. If she made an overture towards me I wouldn't be rude or unkind, not like she'd been to us, but would answer her briefly. Looking back I can now see it probably wasn't totally her fault she was like it; it was just on account of his being so aggressive towards everyone.

One day, just Rob was at home when Aunt Lil turned up unexpectedly to do some chores. She busied herself in the kitchen but found some stains in the sink which proved especially difficult to shift. So she decided to use a tried-and-tested method commonly used at the time and mixed some paraffin with water, (which had been used to degrease aircraft during the war).

She used the mixture on the sink and managed to remove most of the stains then, when she'd finished, she tipped the remaining mixture down the loo, and made herself a cup of tea, congratulating herself on a job well done.

A short while later, he came in, grunted a brief greeting to aunt Lil then immediately went off downstairs, taking his newspaper and cigarette, and heading for the loo.

He settled himself down for a long relax on the loo, paper in hand, before taking out a fag and lighting up. He finished the fag before his business had been completed, and then of course he had to get rid of the dog-end. Not wanting to get off the loo, he bent forwards and threw the fag end into the pan behind and underneath him, while still sitting on it.

My brother, Rob, told us later that he'd heard one almighty 'Whoosh!' as the cigarette combusted in the paraffin and sent up flames. Since he was sitting back on it by then the flames covered his rear end and consequently burned his bum severely. Apparently, although none of us, naturally, asked to see the damage, he was actually burnt quite badly and his entire derriere became covered in blisters.

He went mad at his sister, who protested that she was only trying to help out. His reaction was, of course, in complete contrast to ours as we all thanked her profusely. In fact I think, looking back, which was the moment when I decided Aunt Lil wasn't so bad after all!

Rob reported back that his crotch was painful for months afterwards and he walked like John Wayne for about six months...Yippee!!

Just a pity it wasn't permanent!

John

When John was about twelve years old, he used to help the old man on his fruit and veg barrow stall which he ran outside the pub. He made John stay away from school to help do this so John lost a lot of schooling; he also missed all the holidays we had with Cyril and Pat.

The School Board was always after him and one teacher in particular used to really take it out on him by hitting him from behind. That teacher nearly got John expelled too.

John was very honest and would never overcharge or cheat anyone. Despite this, one evening, after checking the cashbox, the old man accused John of taking some money from it.

John denied it but the old man gave John a good hiding anyway.

'Now get outta the house!' he said and turfed John out, telling him not to come back before morning.

Then he told Mum not that John was in trouble and under no circumstances was she to let him back in that night. All the rest of us were furious and worried to death about John, especially as he had

116

nothing covering him but his old coat. You can imagine how we felt when we found out the next day that John had slept in a shop doorway.

When I remember this I feel just as angry and upset as the day it happened: John was only young , about the same age as my grandson is now, and certainly not safe to be on the streets alone and frightened.

Imagine how we all felt when the money turned up and the old Man didn't apologise, just said he'd 'found' it.

Because he was so honest and the old man never paid him a penny for his help, John didn't have any money. It was coming up to Christmas so they were selling Christmas trees.

'Put some on and sell 'em for more', I said.

'Nah, can't do that; wouldn't be fair'.

'As long as the old man gets what he wants for them, you just add ten bob (equivalent to 50p today), to each'.

So John did and he made quite a nice little amount which he spent on Christmas presents for everyone else of course.

When John was around fourteen, he met Carol, the girl who later became his wife. Her name was Carol Taylor and she was a big fan of jiving: that was the craze at the time. Carol used to go to the milk bar with her friend Daphne and John met her one evening at the bus stop.

'You shouldn't go home on your own'.

'I'm alright'.

'I only live in Sherland Road so I'll take you back'.

So after that they started seeing each other.

Sometime later Carol took John home to her flat to meet her parents.

'Hello Mrs Taylor, Mr Taylor', he said, being a polite lad and wanting to make a good impression.

'So you're John....welcome lad', Mr Taylor said to him.

After that John was a frequent visitor but, although he went a lot, he always greeted them in that formal way.

One day when he arrived, the woman who lived in the flat below said, 'You tell that Jimmy Smith: wait till I get hold of him'.

John said 'I don't know no Jimmy Smith!'

'What! You bin going on with his daughter for months!'.

Apparently Jimmy Smith was the bloke John had been addressing as 'Mr Taylor': he was Carol's stepfather but no one had told John and he'd been going round there for months!

When John went in, he didn't want to disrespect Jimmy so he bit his tongue and, instead of saying 'OK Mr Smith?', which he wanted to do, John just looked and said nothing.

Jimmy realised John knew so he said: 'Just call me Pop'.

John and Carol were courting as we used to call it, for six years. Then one day out of the blue, Carol dumped him. John didn't tell us straightaway but we soon realised when he didn't speak about Carol any more and didn't go out in the evenings and eventually he said 'I'm not with her no more'.

But they still used to bump into each other from time to time.

One day Carol asked him: 'What you doing tomorrow?'

'Nothing'.

'Come round to dinner then'.

'Well you'd better ask your Mum and Dad',

Carol said,'I've asked them already!'

After that they got engaged but theirs was always quite a volatile relationship.

I remember one dramatic argument when Carol took her engagement ring off and threw it at John: he then chucked it out the window.

Of course, as soon as it had gone they both realised what they'd done. It was Jim who had the bright idea that found it though.

'Chuck something else out and see where it lands'.

So they did ….and Jim went outside and found the ring!!

I've always been very proud of John because of the way he was treated by the old man but I realise now that was true of all of us: we all managed to come through despite having such a nasty, cruel and vicious bastard of a father. We even all grew up reasonably sane but that was down to our wonderful Mum and the amount of laughter we had in our lives.

Despite losing so much school time, John got a very good job 'in the print' which paid top money and was a very secure, respected job. He made a happy marriage, even if it got a bit dramatic at times with their arguments, and he ended up with a very nice house.

Sadly, when she was in her early sixties, and after over forty years of marriage, Carol died in his arms: she'd been ill with cancer and had gone back to the hospital to receive the 'all-clear' that she was in remission, when she turned to John, said 'I'm feeling tired', and fell into his arms.

John and I are still close and, to this day I still feel protective towards him: I know we'll maintain our close relationship until the day we die.

Cyril's MBE

My brother-in-law, Cyril, was quite an amazing man.

He did a lot for charity, especially children's charities, but very few people knew of this, apart from close friends. He also helped some famous people like Spike Milligan and Harry Secombe, and some well-known footballers and together they raised enough money for one of the very first laser eye treatment machines.

He raised money for the children's hospital so that children, who'd never been to the seaside even though they were over twelve years old, could go on a nice holiday.

He used to supply the local schools with Christmas trees and boxes of fruit, and made sure the elderly had coal in their cellars.

Because of his outstanding efforts over the years, Cyril was awarded the MBE by the Queen. Although this was such an honour, Cyril was greatly embarrassed as he was such a modest man.

By the time my sister, Sadie, died, Cyril had a kind of dementia, so his children sold the family home and put all the money into the very finest residential Care Home they could find for him.

121

He had a large room with many of his personal possessions which they brought from home and the main lounge in the Home was very comfortable with lovely sofas and nice upholstered chairs which weren't plastic. The grounds were also amazingly well-tended and they had entertainment rooms and exercise rooms.

But the best thing was the fact that the air was clean and fresh-smelling, no lingering smell of cooking as all the (lovely) food was sent in.

He had visitors every day of course.

When Cyril developed cancer later, his children made sure he had the very best private treatment which, of course, meant he could go straightaway, no waiting.

He was my sons' role model and an amazing human being: a beloved husband, father, grandfather, friend, son and sibling.

My young life was sad and scary most of the time but also very rich in special people and full of surprises and contrasts. It had evil in the old man but great goodness in Mum, Cyril, Pat and others around.

And how many families can boast of a family member with an MBE?!

Jim's Stay in Hospital

This is really about how I think I'm so complex in my humour as what some people find funny, I don't.

Jim was admitted to hospital to have two benign tumours removed from his lower back.

We all took it in turns to visit him except, of course, you know who.

Opposite Jim in the ward was an elderly man in to have his leg amputated.

I went to see Jim after his (successful) operation and he told me, quite casually, that the man opposite had had the wrong leg taken off.

I was so very sad for him but most people laughed when I told them as they thought it was really funny, almost a joke.

Don't be embarrassed if you smile or laugh: most people do except me.

Afterthoughts

Looking back, from when I was around three, my life was just one nightmare of violence and shouting. The kitchen was constantly being disturbed by the table and chairs being tipped over, the window wide open with him shouting to the neighbours:

'Do yer fuckin wanna listen to all this?'

When I was a little girl I would sit on my Mum's lap till he came in but as soon as he arrived home he'd pull me off and hit her.

'What the fuck's she doing up late?'

I can also remember thinking from a very young age that it must be nice to be very old and living on your own in a little house of your own. No screaming and fighting. I now have that and I'm very happy with what I've got. I'm so proud of both my sons and I love all my grandchildren to bits.

I'm glad I married my first husband because of the sons I've got: I wouldn't have had it any other way. I still miss my Mum and my sisters very much: Mum was the best thing in my life, ever, and both my sisters felt a massive part of it too. Pat was special as she was always my role model but Sadie and I went through so much together.

I now live in a nice house which, though it's small, is warm and well-maintained and I have my family living near.

I'm lucky: I survived and I can honestly say 'Love shone through' in the end.

Jackie

Printed in Great Britain
by Amazon